Across
the River

ALSO BY ALICE TAYLOR

MEMOIRS

To School Through the Fields
Quench the Lamp
The Village
Country Days
An Irish Country Christmas

POETRY

The Way We Are
Close to the Earth
Going to the Well

FICTION

The Woman of the House

ESSAYS

A Country Miscellany

DIARY

An Irish Country Diary

CHILDREN'S

The Secrets of the Oak

Alice Taylor

Across *the* River

St. Martin's Press
New York

www.stmartins.com

ISBN 0-312-27843-8

First published in Ireland by Mount Eagle Publications

First U.S. Edition: June 2001

10 9 8 7 6 5 4 3 2 1

To Mike

CHAPTER ONE

MARTHA GAZED INTO the mirror and studied her face with dispassionate appraisal. It must be easier to grow old and lose your good looks if you had been plain all your life. You did not have that much to lose. She knew many plain women who had actually improved with age. They became serene and comfortable-looking, the last thing that she would ever want. She had always stood out in a crowd. Once she had overheard her sister-in-law Kate compare her to a black swan, and when you were used to being regarded as beautiful it was disquieting to observe the glow begin to diminish.

She turned her head and raised her chin to study her side view. Her jawline was not as clean cut or as well defined as it had been. When she lowered her chin, it became more obvious. She angled her face to get a better side view. Her skin was losing its fine clear texture and she could see a few open pores with a slight rough, grainy effect. A short black hair sprouted from the edge of her jawline and she grasped a tweezers and whipped it out. When she stared directly at her face, the fine skin under her eyes was no longer soft and moist but beginning to wrinkle a little like fine tissue paper. She picked out a grey rib from her long black hair and saw a few extra ones since her last examination. She had considered colouring her hair, but on Sundays when she looked up the church and took note of dyed heads she changed her mind.

Since Ned's accident she had dressed in black, first in mourning but later because she knew that it suited her. As well, people dressed in black were unapproachable, and that suited her too. In life people tripped you up and it was a good idea to keep them at a distance.

Kate had remarked that she never walked into a room but swept into it. Although probably meant as a criticism, she had taken it as a compliment. Kate had never liked her and she certainly had no time for Kate, who was a do-gooder with her nose stuck into everything, thinking that she could improve the world. She doubted that losing her looks bothered Kate, but then she did not have that much to lose.

The mirror hung at eye level on the shutter of the kitchen window, and the full glare of the midday light left no room for illusion. Raising her head, she examined her neck. No cause for comfort there either.

Maybe she should begin to take better care of herself. The prospect of growing into a wrinkled old hag or an overweight porker did not appeal to her, but the possibility of either ever happening was remote. Her fine bone structure would withstand well the progress of years, and weight had never posed a problem. There was good physical exercise around the farm and hard work had never bothered her. Life had been easy when Ned was alive; after the accident it had been tough, but she had had no choice but to keep going. Someone had to run Mossgrove. Then gradually she had realised that she enjoyed being in control and that the challenge stimulated her.

Since Ned's death eight years ago, there had been problems on the farm, but she had solved them and had enjoyed the sense of achievement. Many of the neighbours did not like her, but because she was Ned's widow they were all helpful. All of them with the exception of the Conways, who hated her because she was a Phelan. Strange that she had never considered herself a Phelan. They were Ned's family but never hers. Moving into their family home she had felt threatened by them, by the living ones but also by the ones who were gone. Even though they were dead, they seemed to haunt the place in the trees they had planted, their buildings and the things they had made. She glanced with disdain at the huge old dresser that stretched across the entire end wall of the kitchen. It had been made by Edward Phelan, Ned's grandfather.

Over the years she had wanted to throw it out, but everything that the dead Phelans had made was sanctified in the eyes of those who came after them.

Part of that problem was Jack, who had worked Mossgrove with three generations of Phelans and was still here to work with Peter, who would be the fourth generation. Jack kept the dead Phelans alive by constantly talking about them as if they were part of present-day life. It annoyed her intensely, but there was no way that she could change Jack. He was as much part of Mossgrove as any Phelan, and sometimes she felt that he was more part of it than herself. They differed on occasions but over the years had developed a grudging respect for each other. Dislike of the Conways was a common bond between them.

As yet she had not sorted out the problem that the Conways posed along the boundary down by the river, but one day it would come to a head and then she would make her move. There was no way that they were going to get the better of her. Ned had been too soft with them. The bitterness between the families went back to the time of old Edward Phelan, Ned's grandfather, and it had festered ever since, but she was determined that in her time it would be sorted out once and for all. In the mean time there was the more immediate problem of Peter, who was now home full-time to work in Mossgrove.

Peter! The only son, but they had never understood each other. All that rubbish about sons and mothers was not true in their case. Peter and herself had clashed ever since he had first voiced an opinion. If only he were more like Nora, but Peter had always been independent and strong-willed, though that had created no barrier between Ned and himself; love of Mossgrove had been their common bond.

After Ned had died she had gone through a bad patch and had attempted to sell Mossgrove. Peter had never forgiven her for that. He had been twelve at the time, but the whole episode seemed to have been imprinted on his memory. Even though she had changed her mind, Peter was still resentful of what he saw as a betrayal of his father and Mossgrove.

She hoped that he would never find out that her mind had been changed for her because there was a legal reason why Mossgrove could not be sold. She had sometimes wondered if Kate and Jack knew the real truth. If they did they kept their own counsel and never used it against her, but Peter would be different. He was direct and forceful and enjoyed opposing her.

A sudden movement reflected in the mirror startled her. She whipped around to discover Peter leaning against the jamb of the back door, studying her with an amused look on his face. How long had he been there? He must have slipped in quietly while she had been absorbed in her facial appraisal. It irritated her to think that he had caught her at a disadvantage. Typical of him to stand there silently availing of the opportunity to belittle her!

"Surveying the ruins?" he questioned mockingly.

"How long have you been standing there spying on me?" she demanded, sitting on the edge of windowsill, folding her arms tightly and facing him.

"Mother Martha. . ." he began, raising his hands in mock submission. Tall and athletic, when he bent forward in an ironic bow his blond hair fell across his forehead.

"Don't call me that," she cut across him. "You know that it drives me mad, but of course that's exactly why you do it, isn't it?"

"But it kinda suits you," he taunted. "Did no one ever tell you, Mother, that you had the makings of a great dictator. Run the show with no consultation with lesser mortals."

"Oh, for God's sake," she exclaimed in annoyance. Turning her back on him, she pulled the latch of the window and it slid down with a bang. "When someone knows what they're doing, where is the point in running around discussing things with fools?"

"It's called democracy, Mother," he told her evenly.

"Well I call it a waste of time," she declared, returning to the edge of the windowsill.

"That's my mother," he said, still leaning against the jamb of the door and rolling his eyes towards the ceiling.

"Stop acting the smart man now," she snapped. "Just because you were the star turn on the school debating team does not necessarily mean that you have all the answers."

"Well, the way it is now, Mother," he told her with determination, "I did not spend two years in agricultural college to come back here to run Mossgrove the way you have been doing it since Dad died."

"It's as well run now as it ever was," she insisted

"Not saying that it isn't," he told her sharply, and she could hear the supressed irritation in his voice, "but if you intended to continue on as you were, where was the point in sending me to do this agricultural course after my Leaving Cert? I could have done something else if I knew that I was supposed to come back here to act as another Jack or Davy Shine, doing your say-so."

"Oh, so you've been discussing me with Jack and Davy Shine," she accused him.

"Did I say that?" he demanded.

"There you go again," she told him, "with your smart logic, behaving as if you were talking to a dimwit."

"I wonder where did I get that from?" he asked.

"I never talk down to people," she asserted with exasperation.

"Maybe not," he told her sharply, "but you treat them that way, which is far worse."

"Is this conversation about you, me or the farm?" she demanded.

"About all three, I'd say," he told her mildly, "because we're a bit like the Blessed Trinity, aren't we? Inseparable and hard to understand."

"Oh, for God's sake, Peter, will you stop talking rubbish and go out and do something useful instead of driving me mad," she fumed as she strode to the table and began to mix with vigour the cake that she had begun an hour previously.

"That's our mother all right," he told no one in particular as he walked over to the window. "Won't discuss anything, just bulldozes on with the belief that everything will flatten in front of her."

"What is it you want to discuss?" she demanded, resting her hands on the side of the dish.

"Money," he told her, still standing at the window with his back to her and looking down over the farm.

"Oh, so that's it," she said.

"How do you mean, that's it?" he asked over his shoulder.

"Well, everything is about money, isn't it?" she said.

"In your world," he agreed.

"Here we go again."

"No, here we don't go again," He jerked around from the window with an obstinate look on his face. She knew that look since he was a child. "We need to invest in a new milking machine and a new tractor and to bring this place up to date," he told her with determination.

"Have you any idea what kind of money you're talking about?" she demanded.

"Down to the last penny," he informed her decisively, returning to look out the window.

"But more important," she wanted to know, "where is this money going to come from?"

"You have money stashed away somewhere," he told her quietly, "because Dad had money in the bank when he died."

"How do you know that your father had money in the bank?" she demanded in surprise.

"He told me," he said.

"At your age!" she protested. "You were only twelve."

"We talked about everything, and I never forgot one thing that Dad told me. That's Mossgrove money you've got and it has to be reinvested back into Mossgrove."

"Well, I've heard it all now. Mossgrove money," she breathed in anger. "Are you telling me that this valuable land is looking for its own back? You're a bit young to be advising me what to do."

"Dad was only sixteen when his father died and he ran Mossgrove."

"There was no one else then," she told him.

"Oh, by God, there was," he asserted. "Jack told me that he and Nana Nellie ran this place for years before that because Grandfather Billy had lost interest in it."

"And did Jack tell you why your grandfather could not run Mossgrove? Oh, no, of course not. Jack paints perfect pictures of the Phelans. Well, I'll tell you: your grandfather, Billy Phelan, was a drunk and he nearly ran this place into the ground."

"But Nana Nellie kept it going with Jack," he said with pride, "and when Dad was able, they encouraged him and he did a great job."

"But you're not your father," she declared, knowing that it would cut deep. To Peter his father had been perfect and his death had heightened that perfection. Peter stood motionless for a few seconds and when he swung around his face was taut with suppressed emotions.

"No," he said grimly, "and I'm not going to put up with all the shit that he put up with from you."

"You pup," she said, raising her hand to strike him across the face, but he was too fast and caught her firmly by the wrist. He lowered her hand forcibly and pushed it down deep into the lump of dough.

"And you know what a pup's mother is," he told her angrily, his eyes blazing down into hers. He released her hand as if she were distasteful and strode out the door, banging it so hard that the cups on the dresser rattled in their saucers.

Martha paced the kitchen, bristling with rage. Every clash with Peter had this effect. He had the ability to get under her skin and was hell-bent on driving her mad. But it angered her as well that she allowed herself to be so upset by him. She continued to stride up and down the kitchen until eventually her pace slackened and gradually her temper eased. In future she would not allow him to goad her into this state.

She returned to finishing off the cake. Baking, kneading the dough until it became soft and pliable, had a soothing effect on her. With each mould of the hand, her frustration seemed to be absorbed into its soft depths. Working with her hands had always given her satisfaction. Baking, knitting, sewing were all outlets for her creativity, but it was sewing that she enjoyed the most. Hours making curtains, until they were perfect down to the last detail, totally engrossed her.

There had been no curtains on the kitchen windows of Mossgrove until she had come to live here. Now a strong green material framed the two windows, the one at the back looking out into the farmyard and the one at the front looking down over the farm. She had an inate sense of getting it right, and the colour brought the world outside into the kitchen. She had covered the old sofa under the back window beside the fire with the same material as the curtains. The sofa was soft and sagging but very comfortable and had been invaluable when the children were small. Fussy flowery colours did not appeal to her; she preferred the stark and dramatic, so she had painted the kitchen white to see if anything could brighten it up.

Martha had given into the yowls of protest whenever she had threatened to throw out the enormous old dresser, but she had ignored all opposition a few years previously when she had got rid of the open fire and put in an Aga. She had hated the smoke and ashes of the open fire. Jack and the others had prophesied that they would be frozen, but of course with the kitchen warm early and late the opposite was the case. Sometimes people did not know what was good for them. The Aga had set her back a bit, but it had been

19

worth every penny, and when they were doing the plumbing she had put in a bathroom, with a downstairs toilet off the scullery. It had all been money well spent.

Shaking the flour on to the timber table, she flattened out the cake, rounding the edges with the palm of her hand. Opening the top oven of the Aga she eased the cake in and returned to the table where she rubbed her hands together to ease the clinging dough from between her fingers. Now she felt better; the inner turmoil had subsided. She wiped off the table and took the baking utensils out to the sink in the scullery and washed them. When she came back to the kitchen, she went to the parlour to open the window. As she crossed through the small porch, she opened the front door and sunlight poured in.

The parlour was a large low-ceilinged room, and the mirror-backed sideboard against the back wall reflected the lace-curtained window on the wall opposite. The shelved overmantel above the black marble fireplace, to the right of the door, held a collection of family bric-a-brac, school photographs of Peter and Nora and little presents that they had brought home from school tours. On the wall opposite was a large painting of old Edward Phelan. She had never liked this room because the ghosts of former Phelans seemed particularly strong in here, more so since Kate had brought back that painting.

Going over now she stood in front of the portrait and studied it. The original photograph must have been taken when he was well past his prime, but he was still a fine looking man. Kate's conscience must have been bothering her about having taken the old photograph in the first place. Even though Martha might not have hung it up, it still annoyed her that Kate had taken it. Then Kate had got Mark to paint this portrait from it, and he had certainly done a great job, but then that should not have surprised her. Everyone was at great pains to impress her about her wonderful artist brother. She sometimes felt that Mark was more acceptable to the Phelans than she would ever be. Her mother thought that they should all encourage him, so as his sister she had little choice but to hang old Phelan in the parlour. She hoped that one day the twine keeping him up would break and he would crash to the floor in smithereens!

Viewing the parlour as she had so many times in the past, she decided that it could not be made to look well with its low ceiling and the uneven walls. Old houses were impossible, all shadows and corners. She remembered, shortly after coming to live in Mossgrove, looking at this room and all the old Phelan photographs. They had eyed her from every wall, but she had soon relegated them to the cupboard on the upstairs landing.

This was the room where all the big events in the life of Mossgrove were celebrated. Special meals were partaken of in here for christenings, holy communions and confirmations. It was here Nellie Phelan had spent her later years when it was no longer feasible that they share the one kitchen. Here too she had been laid out when she died, and it was back to this room they had brought Ned's body after the accident.

She recalled the first family get-together after his death. She had brought them all in here for a special tea and to tell them that their beloved Mossgrove was safe because she had changed her mind about the sale. If the walls of this old parlour could talk, they would tell the story of Mossgrove and of the generations that had lived and died here.

Returning to the kitchen, she looked out the back window and saw Peter and Jack in deep conversation across the yard. Jack had a serious look on his weather-beaten face as he listened intently to Peter, who was sitting on the grass under the hedge with Bran wedged between his knees. Jack had been edging the blades of the mowing machine, but that operation was suspended while he gave Peter his undivided attention.

After Ned's death he had become Peter's father figure, and Martha knew that he was a listening ear for all Peter's problems. She could guess the topic now under discussion. Peter would be frothing at the mouth with temper and Jack trying to calm things down. But whatever they cooked up between them, they were not going to pour her money into this bloody land. She had other plans for that money.

CHAPTER TWO

J ACK SAT UNDER a tree in the corner of the haggard. He had been able to feel the hot sun penetrating through his tweed cap and overheating his bald head, and the deep shadow beneath the tree had looked cool and inviting. Bran had already decided that it was the place to be on this hot day. *Wasn't it great to have a day so good that dog and man had to be looking for shelter!* He scrope the legs of the cow stool along the ground to make sure that the three legs were on level surface and then put his bag of hay on top. *Always better to take the levels before trusting yourself on a cow stool; never do to finish up with your legs in the air. Now to get down to business.*

He lined up the mowing machine blades against the wall beside him, placing the edging stone and a rusty gallon of water at his toes. Then he settled himself comfortably on the bag of hay. *It's good*, he reflected, *to get yourself properly organised before you begin anything.* He had been trying to drum that into Davy Shine's head for years, but so far it had failed him. Peter, now, was a different man altogether: sharp as a needle, that young fellow, and Davy and himself such good friends. Davy had come here eight years ago when he was twenty and Peter was twelve, and there was no doubt but that he had helped Peter get over the loss of Ned. Davy had lost his own father when he was young, so he understood what Peter was going through. As well as that, Davy had worked in Mossgrove when he was a young fellow going to school, so there was little he did not know about the place. He understood the situation between Martha and Peter very well and of course was totally on Peter's side. Peter could do no wrong in his eyes. *So it is up to me to keep the balance,* Jack thought. *Strange to be in Martha's corner, but if someone does not try to calm things down around the place, they'll have holy murder!*

He remembered once hearing Kate say that if they did not handle Peter properly there could be trouble because he had a lot of Martha and his grandfather, Billy, in him, a volcanic combination. Funny how Martha could only see his grandfather in him and nothing of herself. *There is no doubt about it,* Jack thought, *but we only see what we want to see.* But Peter, like a thoroughbred, would have to get his head or he'd kick the sides out of the stable. Strange that Martha could not see that. If she would only give him a bit of rein, he had the makings of a great farmer. He had tried to tell Martha that, but she was convinced that he had a blind spot where any Phelan was concerned.

Jack was not denying but that he had a great respect for them, which he had first gained from Edward Phelan who had been the head of the household when he had come here as a lad of fifteen, all of fifty-eight years ago. The old man had been mighty but as hard as nails in some ways. His son, Billy, was never designed for farming and Mossgrove nearly slipped from their fingers when he was in charge. But Billy's wife, Nellie, was great, and even though there were times when he thought that it would kill her, she kept the place going. She primed Ned for the job and he put Mossgrove back on its feet. God, he was a mighty loss! When Ned died Jack had thought that they were finished, but Martha rose to the occasion and kept the show on the road. She was no easy woman to work for because given half a chance she would walk all over you. The secret was to avoid confrontation. Peter, however, had no notion of doing that and constantly locked horns with her. He remembered old Edward Phelan once saying, "Sometimes it takes your own to level you". Maybe his words were coming true now.

Jack dipped the edging stone into the gallon of water and worked it along the blade. It gave him immense satisfaction to see the brown froth gather and the steel turn from a dull wedge to a silver edge. He worked his way along the blade, leaving behind him a pointed row of shining steel. *This is a grand job,* he thought, *for a fine day.*

He loved the haggard of Mossgrove. It did his heart good to look around at the fine stone buildings that he had helped to build and the solid timber doors that the old man and himself had hung years ago. Everything that the old man had done had to be perfect.

The bang of the back door crashed him back to reality. *Good God,* he thought, *is Peter trying to bring the bloody door with him or knock down the back wall?* His sight was not what it used to be, but he could still read the danger signals across the yard. The scratching hens squawked in protest and ran for cover as Peter kicked a path through them. Bran, who had been stretched out in the shade, anticipated trouble and gathered himself to slip behind Jack. *Sound dog, Bran,* Jack thought. Peter was fond of him, but Bran was taking no chances.

Peter kicked a big stone across the yard and it bounced off the wall beside Jack, bringing a shower of loose stones cascading down.

"Easy, lad," Jack soothed, "or you'll kill someone."

"I know who I'd like to kill," Peter breathed through clenched teeth as he threw himself on the grass beside Jack: "that jade of a woman inside."

"That wouldn't solve much," Jack said easily.

Peter threw his eyes to heaven and slapped his hands together.

"Sometimes, Jack, you drive me bloody mad, you're so goddamn reasonable," he complained.

"It takes years." Jack smiled, waiting for Peter to wind down. Peter lost the head easily but usually cooled down quickly enough.

Bran rested his snout on his paws under the cow stool and looked out enquiringly at Peter where he lay on the grass. After a few minutes, when Peter sat up and started to chew a sop, Bran judged it safe enough to emerge from behind Jack. He slunk over to Peter with his tail between his legs and started to nuzzle into his hand.

"What are you so apologetic about?" Peter demanded, cupping Bran's head in his hands and looking down into his eyes. "You did nothing out of the way."

"He's apologising for the world," Jack told him. "Dogs are the greatest comforters of all."

"It would take more than Bran to bring me right after that episode," Peter told him.

"What was it this time?" Jack asked.

"You know, Jack," Peter began in frustration, "that I have it in my head to get a tractor and milking machine in here to cut down the work and waste of time, and for God's sake, Jack, it's 1960, not the middle ages! Well, when I told herself inside about it she nearly lost her head over it."

"Ah, Peter, don't tell me now that you came out about the two things at the same time?" Jack protested.

"Yerra, for God's sake, Jack, where was the point in

beating about the bush? We need the two of them and that's it, isn't it?" Peter demanded.

"And you finished up with neither."

"I'm not beaten yet."

"Listen to me now, my lad," Jack instructed. "Going in there demanding what you did off your mother in one go would be a bit like Fr Brady telling you when he is lining you up to take a penalty that he wanted you to score two goals instead of one. You couldn't do it and neither could she."

"Jack, that's the strangest comparison I ever heard," Peter told him, but a smile started to spread across his face. "Do you think that my mother has the makings of a full forward?"

"God help the backs," Jack smiled.

"She'd never stick to the rules." Peter grinned, amused at the whole concept. "She'd kick a fellow on the ground and abuse the referee and lead her team off the field."

"But she'd never score an own goal," Jack declared.

"That's for sure," Peter agreed. "She'd have it all figured out in advance. She is what Fr Brady calls a strategist."

"Now you have it, lad," Jack told him, "and you must play her game and dodge ahead of her with the ball, not try to blow it through her, because she'll block you down every time."

"Jack, you're a wily old devil."

"I've survived here for over fifty years," Jack smiled.

"I'd never have done that if I was a 'Johnny Head in Air'."

"Dad used to recite that poem."

"Maybe he was telling you something."

"Maybe," Peter agreed, "and now that I come to think about it, you are a lot like Dad or he like you. I'm not sure what way around that should be."

"Either way will do," Jack told him. "I suppose in many ways I had a lot to do with the rearing of your father."

"And me too."

"And yet you're very different."

"Do you think so, Jack?" Peter asked in a troubled voice, and Jack realised that he was treading on sensitive ground. *Herself inside must have done the devil about the Phelans*, he thought.

"Well, yes and no," Jack told him. "You have his clear thinking and you'll make a great farmer just like he was, but you don't have his patience. But then he did not get that from old Edward Phelan. A mighty man but would walk over you if you came in his way."

"He's the one who had the tangle with the Conways, wasn't he?" Peter asked.

"He was indeed," Jack agreed

"Tell me about that again," Peter asked thoughtfully. "Dad told me a long time ago, but I'm not so sure I understood it at the time."

"I'll give it to you short and precise now, lad," Jack said. "Your great-grandfather, Edward Phelan, and

Rory Conway across the river grew up together and were great friends. Conway got into financial difficulties and your great-grandfather secured him in the bank for a loan. When Conway got out of the financial hole, instead of paying back the loan he bought land at the other side of the hill with the money. Edward Phelan was left holding the baby, but not for long. He went and measured the piece of land that Conway had bought and then fenced off the exact same amount of Conway land along his own boundary by the river and took possession. There was a court case and your great-grandfather won and got those two fields, but they have caused trouble ever since."

"But wasn't it strange that those two fields ever belonged to the Conways in the first place, because they are at our side of the river? It would make more sense if they were our land because the river is usually the boundary."

"That was probably the case away back, because my father always said that the Conways moonlighted those fields off the Phelans when that kind of thing was going on."

"In ancient times," Peter said.

"But not forgotten."

"The young crowd don't want to remember any of that kind of thing."

"Not always wise," Jack advised, "because if you know the seed and breed of a crowd, you'll have a fair idea what to expect from them."

"Do you really think so, Jack?"

"Well, I wouldn't take it to extremes now," Jack cautioned, "and there are exceptions to every rule, but usually you don't get apples off a crab tree."

"If it was properly pruned, Jack, you might," Peter laughed.

Just then they heard the sound of hooves and the pony and cart came into the yard with Davy Shine sitting on the setlock. His smiling round face under a pudding-bowl haircut was aglow with good health. When he saw Peter and Jack sitting in the corner, he shouted across at them, "Ye two lazy bums dossing in the shade and me and poor Paddy here dead from work." He guided the pony over close to them and whipping off his cap he aimed it at Peter. Peter ducked and the cap hit Jack, who shot it back at Davy, getting him on the side of the head.

"Bad job," Jack laughed at him, "when an old fella like me has a better aim than a young lad like you. You can't be much good on the football field."

"We'll give you a place on the Kilmeen team," Davy teased.

"Is there training tonight?" Peter asked.

"There is, so get up off your bum, young fellow, and help me get these churns out of the cart so that we'll get finished early this evening. This is no time for lazy lumps sitting in the sun," Davy said as he pulled the reins and guided the pony over to the milk stand, scattering hens before him.

31

"That's no way to talk to your elders and betters," Jack called after him.

"I'd agree about the elders whatever about betters," Davy shouted back. "Are you going mowing after dinner, Jack?"

"Why do you think I'm edging the blades — to go shaving?" Jack asked him.

Peter laughed and jumping to his feet he ran across the yard to help Davy, his bad humour forgotten. Jack watched them unload the churns out of the cart: Peter tall and blond, Davy dark and blockier. Peter played full forward on the Kilmeen team and Davy full back, and Jack thought that the two positions suited their personalities. They were good lads and he was fond of the two of them, but it was Nora who was the light of his life. *As I get older,* he thought, *it is good to have the young around me. They keep the life in me.*

After the dinner Davy rounded up the two horses while Jack oiled the mowing machine from the long nozzled can. As he replaced the can, he checked that he had all the wrenches he might need in the box of the machine. Never do to have a breakdown with no tools to get going again. As he straightened up he heard the clattering of horses hooves and Davy led James and Jerry, dancing with energy, into the haggard.

"It's easy to know that it's the first day's mowing," Davy declared as they tackled them to the mowing machine. "These two are ready for action."

Jack clambered into the iron seat, secured his bag of

hay beneath him and then guided the horses towards the gate. The wheels made a noisy journey out of the haggard with the blade section standing upright beside him.

"By God, Jack," Davy told him, standing back in admiration, "you're like a fellow driving a chariot. Ben Hur isn't in it with you."

"Out of my way now, lad, or I might mow you down."

"Don't get carried away," Davy laughed. "I might come in handy again. The gates are open down along and I'll be down after you."

Once he got on to the soft sod of the Moss field the journey was smoother. Jack loved the feeling of heading off down the fields to start the first mowing of the season. The furze bushes were a blaze of yellow over in Conways' and the whitethorn was pouring off the ditches into the dykes beside him. He had lost track of the number of years that he had come down these fields at the beginning of summer to begin the mowing, and always it lifted his spirits. *God's in his heaven,* he thought, *and all is right with my world.* He turned into the big meadow along by the river and raised the lever to let down the long blade. *Now, Jack my man,* he thought, *this will test your edging.* The blade cut through the hay like a hot knife through butter. *You have not lost your touch, old man,* he told himself.

As he guided the horses around by the headland, he viewed with satisfaction the tall meadow grass. Different hues of delicate browns and yellows blended together. As the first cut fell the whiff of purple clover filled the air and the smell that wafted up to his nostrils told him that the field was just right for cutting. The horses had their own rhythm and hardly needed him, they were so used to their job. He relaxed on his seat to the soft drone of the mowing machine.

As Jack circled around the field, the island of hay in the centre grew smaller and the swards stretched out around it. He decided that Davy must have forgotten his promise to come down after him to rake out the dykes. That was not surprising, because Davy could be depended on to come across something else that he'd decide had to be done. He might bring down the tea later and stay on then for a while before the cows, or Martha herself could come if she decided she needed to get out of the house. It would give him a chance to put in a good word for Peter, not that she'd listen, but it was always worth a try.

But it was Nora who finally came through the gap swinging the gallon of tea. She was probably just back from school. It did his heart good to see her dancing over the swards, her mane of blond curly hair shining in the sun. With her long elegant limbs she always put him in mind of a well-bred colt. Not a trace of Martha there, nor was she a Phelan either; she was her grand-mother's side of the house and they were easy, gentle people. She often calmed the waters between Peter and Martha. Next year would be her last in the sec-ondary, and if she went further afield, which she probably would, there would be no peacemaker in the house.

"Jack," she called, "do you want to take the horses down to the bottom of the field and we can eat by the river?"

"Grand job, girlie," he said, reining the two horses in that direction and raising up the blade so that they could move more freely. The horses sensed a rest from work and strained forward on the reins. When they reached the lower headland, he eased himself off the seat.

"Getting old and stiff, Nora," he told her, bringing the bag of hay off the seat and placing it on the ground. "You sit there now, girlie, and make yourself comfortable."

"No, Jack," she told him, taking the bag of hay and placing it on the low stone ditch, "you sit here and I'll sit on this big flat stone. It's grand and warm from the sun."

He put a few swards of hay under the heads of the horses, and they crunched noisily with long green strings dribbling from their jaws. Nora and himself settled themselves comfortably on the low ditch overlooking the river.

"Isn't it lovely to listen to the water?" Nora said, looking down through the overhanging branches at the river gurgling over the brown stones beneath them. Then, taking the cover off the gallon, she handed him a cup out of the basket.

"Boys, but I need this." Jack sighed with relief as the tea hit his parched throat.

"I brought a cup for myself as well," Nora told him, "but I'll wait and have my tea when you are having Mom's apple cake because I'm only just after my dinner."

"Your mother's a mighty baker," Jack said appreciatively as he sank his teeth into the nutty brown bread.

"She's great, isn't she?" Nora agreed. "Mom does everything perfectly."

"That's about the cut of it." Jack agreed. *No problem there!*

"Did herself and Peter have a row today?" Nora asked tentatively.

"What makes you say that?" he asked cautiously. He knew that Nora worried about the rows between her brother and mother, so the less she knew about some of them the better.

"I could feel it when Peter and Davy were in for their tea just now, so I decided to come down and have mine with you."

"They had a bit of a scrape all right, nothing much. But you were right to come down here for the tea. Nothing beats tea in the meadow on a sunny day."

"It's lovely here, isn't it?" Nora sniffed the air with delight, looking around at the sheltered meadow and across the river. Then he saw her expression change and he followed her glance. Standing on top of the high bank at the other side of the river, leaning on the fence, was Matt Conway. He was too far away to read his expression, but Jack doubted if it were friendly.

"He frightens me," Nora whispered.

"So he should," Jack told her. "Keep far away from him."

"Why is he standing up there staring down on us?" Nora asked uneasily.

"Trying to make us feel uncomfortable," Jack told her. "He believes in the silent treatment. They say that he hasn't spoken to that poor unfortunate wife of his for years."

"Why has he fencing around the top of the high bank? Nobody could cross up there anyway."

"He put that up when a cow fell down over that bank and got drowned. That's a fierce hole down there, some kind of a whirlpool in it, and whatever goes down never again comes up."

"When we were small, Mom was always warning Peter and myself to keep away from yalla hole."

"And she was right."

"Why do we all call it Yalla Hole?" Nora asked.

"I suppose because the cliff yawning over the water is mostly of yellow mud, so the water in the hole beneath has a yellow reflection."

Nora shivered and then decided. "Jack, let's turn our back on Matt Conway and enjoy our apple cake."

"Sound idea," Jack agreed, and they came down off the little ditch and sat under the whitethorn in the headland. They ate in companionable silence, both busy with their own thoughts. Jack liked the way Nora could sit in silence; few young ones could do that. Peter and Davy were always chewing the cud about something.

When they looked across the river again, Matt Conway was gone.

CHAPTER THREE

Matt Conway sat at the top of the table chewing his food noisily, his eyes half closed in concentration. Wisps of foxy hair were plastered across his bald head and folds of chins rose and fell with each chew as grease oozed out of the side of his mouth and trickled down their furrows. Every so often his jawbone made a clicking noise.

Danny watched him out of the corner of his eye. If he were caught looking at him, he could get a belt across the head. Sometimes Matt Conway pretended to have his eyes closed, but he was only laying a trap, and when he had given Danny a good blow he would roar laughing at the joke of having caught him out. But it wasn't pleasant laughter: it was a derisive bellow with a manic ring to it. Sometimes Danny was convinced that his father was half mad and at other times that he was completely mad.

There was nobody living at home now except himself and his mother. They were all gone, couldn't stick the old fellow. He was not sure how long more he could stick him either. To be treated like a fool and get a blow if you protested was hard to take when you were nineteen, but he could not leave his mother on her own. The old fellow could kill her. He had nearly succeeded a few times.

She had shrunk over the years. It was as if the less space she took up the better her chance of escaping attention. His father's attention meant a battering or a nod of his head towards the foot of the stairs. His mother would have no option but to comply with a cowed look on her face. As a child he had sometimes listened to the rocking of the bed upstairs. He remembered the day that his father had discovered the pills his mother had got from Dr Twomey so that she would have no more babies. He threw her down the stairs, roaring like a lunatic, "You know that it's against the will of God to take those bloody things."

His mother lay in a heap on the floor at the foot of the stairs and his father came thundering down and kicked her.

"Well, what's your explanation? Are you trying to get me into hell with you?"

With blood trickling from her forehead, Biddy Conway had pulled herself up by the banister of the stairs.

"I asked Fr Brady and he said that it was all right," she told him.

"That fella!" he yelled. "That cur isn't a proper priest at all, stuck in there in Kate Phelan's every chance he gets, probably using them himself. You go to Burke in future, he's a proper priest. Do you hear me?"

"I hear you," she agreed resignedly.

Sometimes his brothers had tried to interfere, but the old fellow was as strong as a horse and could beat hell out of any of them. Maybe if Rory and Tom had stayed they could have taken him on together, but Rory had said that if he stayed he would kill him and finish up in jail. Rory had the temper of the old fellow, so maybe he was right to get out.

Danny missed the lads, but it was the girls he missed most, especially Kitty. She was a year younger than him and they had been great pals. She was gone eight years now and had never come back. Mary was gone longer, but then she had been older and he could only just remember her. She had looked so different when she came home for their grandmother's funeral, and it was then that Kitty had gone with her. He could not understand it at the time. Now he could. It was his father, but their reason for leaving was a different one from that of the boys. The thought of it made him squirm with disgust.

"They are working in our meadows," Matt Conway growled.

"I know," said Danny, who knew that the remark was addressed to him because his father had not spoken to his mother for years.

"This could be the year that I might straighten them out," he threatened. He put his large beefy hands on the edge of the table and pushed his chair back, driving the table forward until it banged against Biddy Conway's leg. Danny saw her flinch with pain, but her face remained impassive. His father stretched himself and then pulled up his sagging pants, but his overhanging stomach was too great a barrier to overcome.

"You brush out from those pigs," he barked at Danny and plodded out of the kitchen with his head thrust forward and his hands resting on his backside.

There was silence for a few minutes. Danny watched the window, waiting to see that he had passed before asking his mother, "Are you hurt?"

She raised tired eyes and looked across the table at him. "Not much," she said resignedly.

"He'll be like a devil now while the Phelans are in the river meadows," Danny said. "Every year he goes off the head at this time."

"If it wasn't the Phelans it would be something else," she sighed. "I sometimes think that there is a demon eating him up inside."

Danny was surprised that she was so forthcoming. Usually she said little. Plucking up his courage, he asked, "Why did you ever marry him?"

At first she looked amazed that he had asked the question. She sat very still for a few seconds and then appeared to come to a sudden decision.

"There wasn't much choice," she told him. "I was expecting a baby."

"But how did you come to be mixed up with the likes of him at all?" he persisted.

"Young and stupid," she said bitterly. "Hard to imagine it now, but I could not believe my luck that he even noticed me. He was a fine looking fellow then. A grand dancer. I was actually impressed by his dancing! That's what a fool I was."

Then it was as if, having taken the lid off, she now wanted to let it all out.

"The night that it first happened I could not stop him because he was much stronger than me, and of course when it happened once there was no stopping him. When I told him I was expecting his child, he told me that I was trying to trap him."

"So why did he marry you if he didn't want to?" Danny probed.

"Because my father came to his mother and they patched something up between them. He was afraid of her. She could put a brake on him. Even though she was hard to live with, I missed her when she died, for there was no one to put a stop to him then."

"She got Kitty and Mary out, didn't she?" he asked quietly.

"You understand about that too," she said grimly.

"Why did you never leave?"

"Where was I to go?" she asked resignedly.

"You could have gone to Dublin with the girls."

"I wanted them to have a fresh start and not be dragging me after them. As well as that, if I went up there he might have come after me. I wanted the girls to be safe."

For years he had wondered why the girls did not write, until one day when his father was gone to the creamery. From his bedroom window he had watched his mother go across the fields in the direction of Sarah Jones'. When she came home, he had asked why she went to Sarah's that early and she warned him not to mention it in front of his father. Then she told him about the letters. Mary wrote to Sarah Jones and Kitty wrote to Kate Phelan. She went over to Sarah's to read them and then burn them for fear of their father finding out.

Danny wanted to know why she had never told himself about the letters, but she assured him that the less he knew the less could be beaten out of him. He knew that if his father knew they were in contact through Kate Phelan there would be hell to pay, but it was great to know that Kitty had not forgotten them. Kitty was doing her Leaving Cert this year and Mary was teaching now and earning her own money. It was a great comfort to his mother that they were both independent. Their grandmother had financed the girls for years with the money she made out of the "cure". She had never told anybody about her business, and when she died her brewing secret went with her. Danny often wondered how she had managed to keep it all under control.

"Grandmother must have been an amazing old lady. To think that she could keep himself in his place and he can belt a big fellow like me around is strange, isn't it?"

"No one got the better of old Molly," Biddy told him. "She made the cure for years and no one knew where she made it."

They both sat silently remembering old Molly Conway.

Her next question took him by surprise. "Did you never think of leaving, Danny?"

"I did, but the thought of you being here on your own stopped me."

"You were always a good child," she said, and then continued in a questioning voice, "Isn't it strange, Danny, that we did not have a talk like this before?"

"I was always nervous of asking you questions in case I'd upset you," he said.

"I hadn't realised how grown up you are. When I was your age I was married with a child and another on the way and knew that I'd ruined my life. You must be very careful, Danny, and make the right decisions. I'm always writing that to the girls."

"Where do you write to them?"

"Over in Sarah Jones'. I am very careful; it would be a disaster if he found out where they were."

"Isn't it strange that it's Kate Phelan is your link with Kitty?"

"Could you imagine what would happen if himself found that out? He'd kill me."

"I can just barely remember her being here the night Nana died, and Kitty went with her that night," he said.

"Well, she's the district nurse. She was attending your grandmother when she got blood poisoning in her leg. In some odd way the two of those understood each other. That drove himself mad. Fr Brady was with Kate Phelan that night, so he has it in for him since."

"I suppose if Ned Phelan hadn't died, the problem with the Phelans might have been solved, because he was a very quiet man," Danny said.

"I don't know," she sighed, "but whether it would have been or not, there is no way now Martha Phelan and himself are going to come to any agreement."

"She is a tough woman," Danny said with a hint of admiration in his voice. "She is doing a great job over there, isn't she?"

"She was always an able lady," his mother said. "I remember her in school and you couldn't frighten her."

"I'd say that hasn't changed, but didn't she get a notion of selling after Ned dying?" he asked.

"She did, and when she changed her mind about that it drove himself mad. To get his hands on Phelans' is his life's ambition."

"For all the use he'd make of it," Danny said bitterly. "He is a wash-out of a farmer. If he might run this place properly instead of watching the Phelans across the river . . . He wastes more time down there leaning on top of that stake looking across at them. Is he trying to intimidate them?"

"There is no way that he is going to frighten Martha Phelan. He has met his match in her. Of course, Jack Tobin is over there so long now that he takes no notice."

"It's all so long ago, wouldn't you think that it was time to forget about it?"

"Some things are never forgotten around here," she told him, "especially if it has to do with land or money."

It had startled him to hear his mother talk of being in school with Martha Phelan. That would make them about the same age and yet his mother seemed years older. He looked across the table at her with pity. Her hair was grey and wispy over a small drawn face, and there was a hopelessness about the very way she was slouched on the chair. He thought of Martha Phelan as she swept up the centre isle of the church every Sunday. It was hard to keep your eyes off her. She was magnificent. But the one who reallyheld his attention every Sunday was Nora. Since they had gone to school together in the glen, she had fascinated him.

"You had better go out to the pigs, Danny," his mother broke into his thoughts, "or he'll be up from the river and roaring like a bull."

"You're right," he agreed, rising from the table. "I'm so glad that we had this talk though; it makes things easier."

"It does indeed, and maybe we should have had it before now, but I was not sure you'd understand."

Alice Taylor

As he walked across the yard to the pigs' house, he looked around, and the sight depressed him as always. The farm sheds were a decrepit looking collection of rusty galvanised sheeting with some gaping holes. *If I was in charge around here,* he thought, *there would be a total change.* But what a hope he had. The old fellow held a tight rein and made all the decisions without discussion.

Then he thought back over the conversation with his mother. Wouldn't it be lovely to visit Kitty and Mary? But what about his mother? It would be like abandoning her to leave her here with the old fellow. Imagine his mother going out with a fellow because he was a good dancer! She mustn't have had a spark of sense.

When he opened the door of the pigs' house, rats ran out of the feeding troughs in all directions. God, he hated to see them. The old fellow had a fascination with rats. He set traps and lay the dead bodies out on the dunghill. There was no doubt but that he was a crazy bastard, and Danny hoped that some day Martha Phelan would get the better of him.

CHAPTER FOUR

IT WAS TWO days after her row with Peter before Martha felt like looking at the plans for her new house. She went upstairs and retrieved them from under her bed, took them down to the parlour and laid them out on the table. Before she examined them, she looked up at the picture of old Edward Phelan and smiled. It gave her a certain satisfaction to lay the plans on the table in front of him.

She had made them out herself in an old drawing book of Mark's and for over a year she had worked on them, mostly at nights before going to sleep. Imagining her new house had given her endless satisfaction. It was going to be perfect down to the last detail. She had enjoyed going to bed early so that she could work on the plans without interruption. The time spent on them were the best hours of her day. All the hard work on the farm was going to be worthwhile when the new house would be built. Nobody knew about it yet and she treasured the secret.

She had no doubt but that she was going to have strong opposition. The fact that Peter wanted the money to improve things on the farm would give him powerful ammunition to oppose her, not that Peter needed anything to spur him on where she was concerned. But apart from that, he would be all for clinging on to the old house. Jack, of course, would be horrified and would back him up, and needless to mention that fool Davy Shine would be on their side.

But it was Nora who was the one she would prefer not to upset. Though if it had to be done, it had to be done! Then, of course, there would be Kate putting in her three and fourpence, as if she were still living here. It was a pity that she did not have children of her own, because if she had it might distract her from Mossgrove. She knew that Kate would have loved children, but Martha could not find it in her heart to feel sorry for her. After all, she had everything else: independent job, nice home and good-looking husband who thought she was God's gift to him. How he still thought that, after eight years of marriage to her, amazed Martha. She felt that Kate should be grateful, especially when she thought of the hassle that Peter was causing herself.

Kate would have to mind her own business regarding the house. But, of course, Kate would have Mark and Agnes on her side. It annoyed her the way Mark backed up Kate in any argument against her. Her own brother never supported her! Kate could always wind him around her little finger, and of course Agnes thought that Mark was infallible, so that brought them all together against her.

Kate was the one who had got Mark going with his paintings, and now he was making more money than any of them. The new school that Kate's husband had started had given Mark an opening, and afterwards Rodney Jackson, who had leased them the school building, seemed to have endless avenues for Mark's pictures in America. Everybody seemed to think that Rodney Jackson was God's gift to Kilmeen, and he took it all in his stride. There was something about his calm acceptance of all the good things in his life that irritated her. She remembered that perfectly dressed little boy who had visited his aunts and who had got on so well with Mark, but even then she had been wary of him. Now whenever she met him with Mark he seemed to go out of his way to be charming to her, but she kept him at a distance. Every fool in the parish was falling over him, and she was not going to be one of the crowd. How could somebody who was supposed to be as wealthy as he was spend days rambling around this place and spend hours chatting with anybody who came his way? Granted, he was good-looking, very pleasant and rich, but in her opinion there had to be a catch somewhere. Nobody could be that bloody perfect! All the same, she had to admit he had been a real help to Mark, not that it had made any difference to Mark's lifestyle except that he now seemed to spend all his time painting.

It was the only interest that he had ever had, and as a child it had annoyed her intensely that he was always locked up in his own world where he appeared to be totally happy. Maybe that was why she too became a loner. But they were very different from each other. Mark had no drive, content to spend his life mixing and daubing. It was ironic in one way that what she had most despised about him now provided a regular source of income. He had always been Agnes's white-haired boy and of course she was delighted now that her belief in him had been justified. Why they still lived in that old house when they could have built a better one, Martha could not understand.

She went over the plans again, just for the sheer enjoyment of looking at them. The steps up to the front door would make the house impressive, then the large hallway with the wide sweeping stairway would give a great sense of space. She hated the way you had to come into the kitchen in Mossgrove to go up the stairs that were so steep and narrow. It was like that in all the farmhouses around, except in Nolans' down the road who had built a new house when Tom and Betty got married. Admittedly they had no choice but to build, as there had been no house on that farm, but she always envied Betty Nolan her new house. Now at last she would have one of her own.

She would have two big rooms at either side of the front door and a large kitchen to the back. It would be such a relief to have a fine big back kitchen as well, for all the working clutter. The fact that the house would be so far away from the farmyard would keep every-thing much cleaner, with all the disorder well away from the house. She knew that Peter and Jack would think that it was crazy to be that far away from the yard, but they were simply stuck in a groove. Upstairs, she was going to have four big bedrooms. Every ceiling in this house was going to be high. She had had enough of low ceilings; they gave her claustrophobia.

But her proposed site for the house was going to cause more opposition than the house itself. She was planning to build it in the Clune field, the big field just inside the gate of Mossgrove. It was going to be at the top of the field, facing the road, and she would fence off a good section for a garden and orchard. Jack was so proud of that field, always proclaiming it to be the finest of the farm with the best soil. The thought of los-ing some of it for a house would really drive him mad, but it was her land and she wanted to live up there beside the road.

Some day next week she intended to take the plans over to a builder in Ross and discuss things with him. She could not go local because it would be all over the village and the neighbourhood, and that was the last thing she wanted. Everything had to be right before she broke the news to the rest of them. That should be interesting! When she heard movements in the kitchen, she rolled up her plan and pushed it into the deep drawer of the sideboard.

Peter and Davy were seated around the table and Jack was making tea at the cooker.

"I'll do that," she told him, taking the teapot and going out to the scullery to rinse it.

"We're having a great run of good weather," Jack said with satisfaction as he sat at the table. "We'll be able to save the river meadow tomorrow, with God's help."

"Must be saying your prayers right," Davy told him.

"It wouldn't do you any harm to say a few more, lad," Jack retorted.

"Nobody knows what goes on between a man and his God," Davy proclaimed with a mischievous grin on his face, raising pious eyes to heaven.

"There's not very much going on in your case, and you sitting on the gallery steps last Sunday telling yarns during mass," Jack declared.

"Well, Davy Shine, you should be ashamed of yourself," Peter scolded.

"Weren't you with him!" Jack exclaimed. "Two pagans, enough to bring the rain down and the river meadows not saved yet."

"Jack, is it the fear of the rain or the love of God that takes you to mass?" Peter wanted to know.

"That's enough old guff out of you now, young fellow. As Davy said, what goes on between a man and his God is his own business."

"I'm honoured to be quoted." Davy sighed in mock appreciation.

"What a lot of rubbish you three talk," Martha told them sharply as she poured out the tea. "Are the river meadows ready for saving?"

"First thing tomorrow morning, we'll get going," Jack told her.

"The Conways might come over to help," Peter laughed.

"The Conways are no joke, my lad," she told him sharply.

"Well, they're jokes of farmers," Peter declared. "That place over there is falling down around them and they're years behind the times. That's what happens if you don't keep up to date."

"Did you hear the forecast, Martha?" Jack interrupted hurriedly.

"No," she told him sharply. She knew what he was at all right, trying to head Peter off so that he would not cause an argument, but she was well able to manage Peter without help from Jack. That was the problem with Jack, he thought that he knew the best way to handle everything.

"It isn't equipment that the Conways are lacking," she told Peter, "it's know-how. It's not much good having up-to-date equipment if you don't know what to do with it."

"But could you imagine the great job that could be done if you had the know-how and the equipment?" he asked her.

"Well, they have neither," she told him.

"That's right," he agreed, "and we have only one side of the equation here, because we have the know-how but no equipment."

"There is good farming being done here at the moment," she told him. She could see that Jack, having tried to divert the argument, was now going to keep out of it, and of course Davy Shine was hoping that Peter would get the better of her.

"But we're slipping," he told her. "The Nolans are away ahead of us in the saving of their hay, but of course with the tractor they get things done a lot faster."

"But they don't have as much help as we do," she told him, "so maybe you think that we could do without Davy if we got a tractor and cut down on overheads."

She could see Davy's face turn a deep red as he looked at Peter in consternation. Jack looked out the window as if the view were something that he had never seen before. But Peter was not going to be sidetracked.

"Oh, you're clever, Mother Martha," he taunted, "divide and conquer, but you know that I would never let Davy go."

"But you do not have the right to make that decision," she told him firmly. "I'm in charge here and I do the firing and the hiring, and you would do well to remember that, Davy Shine."

"Didn't say a word," Davy protested in alarm.

"You have no right to threaten Davy like that," Peter said angrily.

"I have every right," she asserted, "and you'd do well to remember that, my boy."

"Come on, Davy," Peter said angrily, getting up from the table and pushing back the chair with such force that it crashed to the floor, "we don't have to sit here and listen to this ranting."

When they were gone Jack and herself sat in silence. The only sound was the ticking of the clock hanging on the wall above them. She could sense his disapproval, but she was not going to give him the opening to start giving advice. Eventually he cleared his throat and said, "He is only a young fellow."

"And a young fellow who's got a lot to learn," she told him sharply.

"Doesn't every young fellow?" he said evenly. "And the only way they learn is by experience."

"Experience keeps a dear school and a fool won't learn in any other," she told him, "but I'm not prepared to foot the bill for his foolishness."

"Peter is a long way from being a fool."

"Sometimes I wonder," she snapped.

"He was one of the best students they had in that farming school, and that head man said that he had great potential," Jack reminded her.

"Book farming," she said contemptuously.

"A bit more than that now; after all they have a fine farm there."

"Easy for them and we all paying for it," she said.

"Well, the young fellows have to learn somewhere."

"Peter's father learned at home."

"But he was very anxious that Peter should have everything that was available."

"I can't spend my life being dicticated to by the dead," she told him. "I'm on the ground here and I have to work with what I have."

"But the Phelans were never behind the door when it came to progress," Jack said.

"I'm not a Phelan," she told him.

"But Peter is," he said, "and if he doesn't get his head he could jump over the traces and be gone."

"Well, so be it," she said firmly.

"Maybe so be it at the moment," he told her, trying to keep the irritation out of his voice, "but what about down the road in a few years time with no young blood around the place, because if Peter goes Davy will go with him, and selling is not an option."

He slipped in the last statement without any change of tone but she got the message.

So Jack knew that she could not sell Mossgrove, and if Jack knew then Kate knew as well, because the only way that he would know was through Kate. They had kept a very tight grip on that bit of knowledge for the last eight years. She had often wondered. Kate must have gone to Old Hobbs the solicitor and found out. So Kate had known even before they had that big spread in the parlour where she had told them all she had changed her mind about selling. God, Kate was some bitch! She must have been smiling up her sleeve all these years.

"So you knew all these years about the provision in Nellie's will that Kate had the right-of-residency here and that I couldn't sell," she said.

"We did," he told her.

"You played your cards very close to your chest."

"No point in upsetting everyone," he said quietly.

"Peter does not know, I assume?" she asked.

"No, and he won't either," he told her, "or at least I hope that he never needs to know."

"Is that a threat?" she demanded.

"No," he said, "but in the heel of the hunt, the future of Mossgrove is at stake and the security of the Phelan family."

"And nothing must come before that," she said bitterly.

"But surely," he reasoned, "something can be worked out to the satisfaction of everyone. After all, a tractor is not going to cost a fortune, and later on the milking machine could be got."

"And where do you think that the money is going to come from?"

"I have never poked my nose into the finances here since Nellie died, because Ned was well able to manage them, but he never made a secret of how things were going; so I would have a fair idea how things are financially here, and I know that we can well afford to get this tractor without breaking the bank."

"Good God," she exclaimed in annoyance, "this place is like living in a glass bowl."

"Martha, be reasonable. Most farmers know exactly how the others are doing. We have only to watch the harvesting and the churns of milk going to the creamery. There are no big secrets."

"So the general consensus is that I have the money?"

"That's right," he agreed and waited for her to make the next move.

"Did it ever dawn on you that I might have other plans for that money?" she demanded, eyes blazing across the table at him.

"But what?" he asked in amazement.

"You will all find out in due course," she told him, getting up from the table and stacking plates with a clatter to indicate that the conversation was at an end.

CHAPTER FIVE

As JACK WALKED up the boreen from Mossgrove to his own cottage, he was deep in thought. Martha had closed the conversation decisively without giving anything away, and when he had met Peter out in the yard afterwards he was like a red devil with bad temper. *Between the two of them you'd want to be God to keep the balance,* he thought. But whereas Peter was all steam and fire, Martha was a dark horse. Sometimes it was very hard to know what she was at. What on earth could she want with the money? Would she have it in her head to buy more land? But that did not make sense because there was no land for sale near them, and sure if she wanted more land she could be working the Lehane place, because her own family, Mark and Agnes, had no interest in farming. It would be Peter's some day anyway because he would probably be the only one for it. Mark never took his nose out of the paints long enough to look at a woman. There was a time when he had thought that Kate and himself might have had something going for them, but that was when they were very young. Just as well that did not work out, because the union of Ned and Martha had been complicated enough without making it a double bill.

The Lehanes were an ordinary run-of-the-mill family. Martha and Mark could have come from different planets. Mark was for the birds, a genius of an artist but not at the races at all. He was on a winner now all right, with Rodney Jackson selling the paintings. Kate was a mighty woman to have brought that about, but then Kate was extraordinary in many ways. They would have no secondary school in the village but for her. She had really sorted out old Fr Burke and wiped out his opposition. The fact that her old friend, Sarah Jones, had a leg of the bishop had made all the difference.

Of course, Sarah had half reared Kate, always down in Mossgrove with Nellie when Billy was drinking and times were troublesome. *There is no doubt but that some of the neighbours around here are mighty, but of course we have the other kind too*, he thought as he turned around and looked across at Conways'. Over the years Matt Conway had made it rough in Mossgrove, and only for Ned being so quiet there would have been real trouble. Matt Conway had opened gates at night and let cows into meadows and let dogs loose in fields of sheep. It had nearly driven him demented, but Ned had held his head and there had been no more court cases. Conway had been quiet since Ned died, so maybe he was after calming down. But he still kept vigil at the fencing stake above Yalla Hole.

When he reached his own cottage at the entrance gate to Mossgrove, Jack stood and looked down over the Clune field. What a great field that was. Old man Phelan used to say you could feed a parish out of a field like that, and he was right. The young wheat was just a few inches tall and there was a green sheen on it right across the field. You could feel the vigour and growth to come. It did his heart good to look at it. The Well field behind it was a good field too, but not as good as the Clune. You could not go wrong in the Clune; any seed you put down there seemed to multiply. As far as the fields of Mossgrove were concerned, it was the flower of the flock.

He closed the gate of Mossgrove firmly behind him and then turned into his own haggard. The hens were locked up for the night, so he knew that Sarah Jones must have been around, but when he went in to the kitchen he found she was still there, sitting by the fire.

"I knew that you wouldn't be long," she told him, "so I decided to wait and have a cup of tea with you."

Sarah must have something on her mind, he decided, *because it is a bit unusual for her to be here this late.*

"Put on the kettle so," he told her as he took off his jacket and hung it on the hook behind the door.

He was always glad to see Sarah, a small, neat, fresh-faced woman with short-cropped grey hair. They had been friends since childhood and had a healthy respect for each other. As the district nurse, she had delivered the whole parish and laid out what was gone of them before Kate came on duty, so Kilmeen had no secrets from Sarah. They were quite safe with her.

Jack sat at the head of the little table and Sarah with her back to the kitchen so that she could enjoy looking out the window down over Nolans' fields.

"There is a great view from this window," Sarah told him.

"There is indeed," Jack agreed, "but this is a cold spot on a windy day. Before the trees grew up, you'd be blown out of it. Mossgrove down below now is like a bird's nest, tucked in at the foot of the hill and still with a fine view down over the glen. That house has the best situation of any around here."

"They had a lot of sites to choose from when they built, away back whenever it was," Sarah said.

"Well, they picked the best," Jack assured her. "The old man did a lot of work on that house when I came here first. It's a fine, dry, sound structure."

"There's a bit of bother down there with you at the moment?" Sarah enquired.

"How'd you hear that so fast?" Jack smiled.

"Peter was in with Kate," she told him.

"Poor Peter," Jack sighed, "blessed and cursed with

the impatience of youth. What he wants, he wants now and not tomorrow."

"So you don't agree with him?"

"Oh, I agree with him all right, but you must cut your cloth according to your measure, and Martha is measuring very carefully at the moment," he told her.

"That's nothing new."

"I know," he agreed, "but the only thing that has me worried is for fear he'll get fed up and bail out altogether. Then we'd be in a real pucker."

"She'd never sell, would she?" Sarah asked.

"No," he told her empathetically.

"You seem very sure."

"I am," he told her. He did not want to say any more because it was not his business to disclose and he was not too sure that he should have let it slip to Martha. However, Sarah took him by surprise.

"It's Nellie's will, isn't it?" she said quietly.

"You knew about that?" he asked in surprise. "Did Kate tell you?"

"No, but I remember Nellie talking about her visit to Mr Hobbs and how he had covered so many eventualities in the will that she was a bit mesmerised by it. So when Martha changed her mind about selling, it was so out of character of her that I thought of Nellie's will and was sure that it had something to do with it."

"Sound woman."

"Did anyone read that entire will?" she asked.

"Well, I don't rightly know," he said thoughtfully.

"Kate was with him, but whether she got to read it all or not I don't know. She was so delighted that Mossgrove could not be sold that she wasn't concerned with anything else. But surely Old Hobbs would have filled her in."

"You must be joking," Sarah told him. "Hobbs would only tell you what you needed to know at any given time. He is second to none but measured, down to the last dot. If Kate did not ask, he did not show."

"And Martha did not go to him at the time," Jack remembered.

"Well, that cooked her goose anyway, because his crowd have always acted for the Phelans and they look after their own."

"I remember Kate quoting him at the time about the making of a will, that it needed to protect the wishes of the dead, the rights of the living and the interests of the unborn."

"Some job that," Sarah smiled, "but Old Hobbs probably succeeded. It might be no harm if Kate called to see him and got the lie of the land."

"Might be an idea," Jack agreed, though he felt that as smart as Old Hobbs was, even he could not have anticipated a problem between Peter and Martha away back before Peter was even born.

Sarah's next question was thrown out so casually that he knew straightaway that it was the reason she had stayed on.

"Hear anything about Kate lately?" she asked lightly.

His heart leapt with anticipation: maybe Kate was expecting. It would be the best news that he could hear.

He knew that not having children was a huge disappointment to her, but of course being Kate she did not make a meal out of it. Time was running out though, and if it did not happen soon they could forget about it.

"She's in the family way?" he asked hopefully.

"'Fraid not, or at least not that I know of," she told him.

"What is it so?" he asked worriedly. It wasn't in Sarah's nature to be hedging around, so it had it be something unpalatable.

"There is a strange rumour going around about herself and Fr Brady," she said quietly.

"What!" he demanded in amazement, and his cup clattered into his saucer. "How could a shagging lie like that get out?"

"Well, the dogs on the street don't have it, but it's there."

"But who has it?" he demanded.

"I think that it came from Julia and Lizzy."

"The two poisonous old bitches," he pronounced with feeling.

"Julia, of course, living across the road from Kate, watches every stir, and Lizzy being Fr Burke's housekeeper has it in for Kate since the trouble about the school, and needless to mention himself had no love for her either," Sarah said.

"How did you come to hear it, because there'd be no way that they'd say that to you?"

"Jim in the post office tipped me off," she told him.

"Good man, Jim, because the sooner this is shot in the head the better," he said. "Are you going to tell Kate?"

"No," she told him to his surprise.

"But how are you going to get around it so?" he asked.

"I think that Fr Brady is the right angle to come at it from," she said slowly.

"Why so?"

"Well, he's always in and out of the house. Kate can't stop him, but he could slow down on the visiting," she said.

"But himself and David are great friends, and he trains the school teams, and they are both caught up in that. It's understandable that he would be in and out of the place and he living up the street."

"I know all that, Jack, but people will talk, and you can't give them anything to say."

"Well, it's a fierce state of affairs when we can't visit each other now without some bitch putting a quare face on it. Is anybody safe from them?" he demanded.

"When you're gone past it like the two of us, Jack, you're dead safe," Sarah told him.

"I'm not sure if that's a comfort or an insult."

"Anyway," she assured him, "the whole thing is no big deal, but I wanted to find out how far it had gone.

If Martha had it, you'd have got a slap of it across the face, so obviously it hasn't got that far yet."

"So you're going to talk to Fr Brady? I don't envy you your job. A fine young man like him who has done more for the young of the parish than anyone we ever had before him. There's a begrudging shower of old whores in there in the village, and all they have to do is tittle-tattle."

"Calm down, Jack; it's the nature of people to talk. I know that this kind of thing drives you mad, but we'll get over it," Sarah told him.

She was right, of course, and when a few minutes later she pulled back her chair remarking, "Better be going, Jack, in case we'd be the cause of scandal," he had to smile in spite of himself.

On his way back from walking with her to the gate, he spotted a few weeds trying to strangle his young cabbage plants, so he brought out his old weeding cushion and got to work. After an hour, when his annoyance had evaporated, he knelt back on his heels and surveyed his cleaned patch with satisfaction.

The following morning he awoke to the sun warm across his face. They were going to have a great day for saving the river meadows. His heart lifted in delight. He had always felt that those few moments before you actually woke up properly and got out of bed were a great barometer of how the day was going to go. How you felt in your gut was the important thing, and he felt that this day was going to be good.

Thank God for that, he thought. *A good start is everything.*

After a quick cup of tea and bite of brown bread, he was on his way down the boreen to Mossgrove. The rising sun was shimmering across the dewy wheat of the Clune field, and the ferns on the ditches of the boreen were clothed in silken cobwebs. What a lot of silent activity went on at night. The sight of these morning cobwebs was magical. He loved the quiet of the dawn fields when he was out alone and monarch of all he surveyed. *Nobody owns this land,* he thought, *neither Martha nor Peter nor I. It belongs to those gone and those coming after us, as much as to us who are here now. It is greater than any of us.*

He rounded up the cows in the field above the house where they were gathered, patiently waiting to be brought in for milking. *Cows are grand creatures,* he thought as he went around and encouraged them to get up. There were the frisky ones who jumped up as soon as they saw you, and they reminded him of Peter, but there were a few Davy Shines in the herd as well that waited until the last minute to disturb themselves. But the sight of Bran bounding across the field brought them hurriedly to all fours.

"Good boy, Bran," he praised as he ran his hand along the bouncing sheepdog's back.

He was on his second cow when Peter joined him with a scowl on his face.

"You musn't have gone to bed at all last night, Jack. Every morning you're earlier."

"How'd you mean, early?" Jack demanded. "With the river meadows to be saved today, sure it's hardly lying in bed I'd be."

"Sure the birds are only just up." Peter sat under a cow further up the house and Jack could hear the milk dancing off the tin bucket.

"The birds have a morning's work done," Jack asserted. "Did you never hear the dawn chorus? They give a recital before they begin their day and that was hours ago."

"I'd say they didn't have a big audience."

"Probably the only time you ever heard it was before you went to bed, and then your sense of appreciation would not be too sharp."

"God, Jack, you're so bright in the morning you are enough to depress anyone. No wonder Davy starts in the other stall so that he doesn't have to be listening to you."

"No trace of him yet then," Jack said. "The mother's gone to her mother for a few days, so there is no one to get him out of bed."

"I gave him a spare alarm clock last night," Peter said.

"'Twould take the Angelus bell to wake that fellow," Jack declared.

Just then they heard the rattle of a bucket and knew that Davy had arrived.

"He'll never start without some smart comment," Jack remarked, and sure enough Davy appeared at the door swinging a bucket and with a milking block propped against his hip.

"Do you know something, Jack," he said solemnly, "before you die we'll patent you and send out replica models and you'd run the country no bother before the rest of us would even be out of bed in the morning."

"And when you die," Jack retaliated, "you'll have contributed so little to the progress of the world that they'll jump on the grave to make sure you won't come up again."

"Oh boys, Jack, that was low," Davy said in an aggrieved tone and disappeared from the doorway.

"Jack, you're not good for the morale in the morning," Peter told him.

"Never mind the morale," Jack said, "there's only one thing on my mind now, and that's getting the river meadow into wynds. So straight after the breakfast as soon as things are tidied up, you and I are going down there, and we must tell Davy to call to the Nolans on his way home from the creamery and tell them what we're at."

"They might be doing something else," Peter said.

"Whether they are or not, the Nolans would never let you down, and Jeremy and Tom would make a big difference to us today," Jack declared.

"Jack, you've tunnel vision."

"Not a bad thing to have because you arrive at your destination faster," Jack asserted and continued, "It will be great to have Nora as well today, because she is as good Jeremy or Davy or yourself."

"Thanks for nothing," Peter said.

"And maybe your Uncle Mark might wander over."

"For God's sake, Uncle Mark is worse than useless, looking at the colour of sops of hay and the shape of frogs legs," Peter protested.

"Never mind, every pair of hands count in a meadow," Jack told him. "It's the one time that I'm all in favour of big numbers, because it's encouraging. There is nothing that would get you down faster than the sight of a large meadow in the flat and facing it on your own. It would pull the heart out of you, and Mark is better than nothing."

"He'd be delighted to hear that," Peter decided.

After breakfast they did the yard jobs, and then Jack dispatched Peter to catch one of the horses and to tackle up the wheelrake.

"Will you do the wheelraking, Peter?" he asked.

"I will, of course, but you usually like to do that yourself."

"I'll come down after you and rake out the dykes that Davy never got around to," Jack told him.

The sun was high in the sky as he walked down the fields with the rake over his shoulder. It was a day to do the heart good. There was no doubt but that June was the best month of the year. A good June and you could be sure of a full barn for the winter. If the weather came fine, the river meadows produced the best hay, that had body and substance and produced a good milk yield. When he reached the field, he bent down and felt the sward. It was crackling dry and ready for saving. It was a joy to be haymaking on a day like today.

He went along by the dykes, raking back the hay into little piles to link up with the rows Peter was making. An occasional frog sprang long-legged over the hay on its way back into the moist dyke. There was no sound but the occasional thump of the wheelrake as Peter dropped the lever after each collection. They worked on steadily and were almost finished when Davy arrived swinging a gallon of tea and a basket.

"Feeding time at the zoo," he called out.

"Are we not going up to the house?" Peter asked in surprise.

"No," Jack told him, "I asked your mother to send down some grub to spare time."

"You're a real slave-driver," Peter exclaimed.

"Did you never hear of making hay while the sun shines?" Jack said. "Well, this is what it's all about, so eat up fast now and let's get started. And before you say anything now, Davy, I want no old guff out of you, only tuck in and get going."

"Wasn't going to open my mouth," Davy proclaimed solemnly.

They had just started on the second wynd when Nora arrived with Tom and Jeremy Nolan.

"Silence please," Davy announced. "Jack is on the rampage and there is no time for talking."

"I'll go along with that," Tom Nolan agreed smiling. "We must make hay while the sun shines."

"Oh my God, not you too," Davy groaned. Turning to Nora he instructed, "Get up on that heap of hay, my girl, and level it out in jig time to see if we can keep this silent order happy."

"Davy, you'd be thrown out of a silent order the first day," Nora told him.

They worked steadily all day, and the wynds rose slowly around the field. The day got warmer and perspiration ran down faces and backs. It was with great relief that they saw Martha arriving laden with a large white enamel bucket and an overflowing basket. Davy was the first to collapse into the nearest heap of hay.

"I was never so glad to see tea in my life," he declared, mopping the sweat off his face with the back of this hand.

They all shared his sentiment, but as soon as they had finished eating, Jack had them on the move again.

"Jack, you're brutal," Davy told him.

"We're going to have all this hay up before the cows," Jack informed him.

It was six o'clock before they put the cap on the last wynd and Jack breathed a sigh of relief. They were a mighty team to work, and the Nolans had made all the difference, as Jack told them.

"Glad to be a help," Tom told him quietly while Jeremy and Peter were testing their fitness in a race up the field.

"We'll do the cows, Jack, if you want to finish up here," Peter called from the gap.

When they were all gone, Jack walked around the field, recapping the wynds and raking down the sides neatly. They were well-made wynds, towering over him and full of golden crackling hay. He loved this time alone at the end of a day in the meadow. The sun had gone low behind the hill sending shadows between the wynds, and it was pleasant to walk around in the cool of the evening. He tied the wynds firmly with binder twine. Now they were safe from any rain and wind that might come. It was a good feeling. In farming you could take no chances with the weather, though he knew by looking at the sky that there would be no break in the weather yet.

He stood at the gap and counted the wynds: fifty in all between the two fields. It was a mighty day's work! He felt satisfaction in every fibre of his being. As he walked up the fields, there was peace in his heart, because when the river meadows were saved the back was broken in providing winter feed for the cows.

CHAPTER SIX

A T FIRST JACK thought that he was dreaming. Then suddenly he realised that there was somebody trying to knock down the front door with frantic thumping.

"What in the name of all that's good and holy is going on?" Jack breathed as he jumped out of bed, stumbled to the door and slapped back the bolt. A half-dressed Davy, gasping from running, nearly fell in on top of him.

"Jack, the bastard is after burning the hay."

"Who? What?" Jack gasped, his mind not able to grasp what Davy was saying.

"The river meadows are on fire," Davy shouted at him. Then he was gone, belting out the path in unlaced boots.

Jack caught the back of the nearest chair to steady

himself. It couldn't be the wynds that they had made yesterday! Was that what Davy was shouting about? *Steady on now, Jack,* he told himself, *take this nice and handy and don't lose your head. If it is what you think it is, there is no good in rushing, because once dry hay starts to burn nothing can stop it. So get dressed slowly and go down there at your own pace and take it easy.* Kate had warned him about taking it easy.

But despite all his instruction to himself, he was dragging on his clothes with a thumping heart. He ran down the boreen, feeling his way instinctively like a cat in the dark. He knew every stone of this boreen, but he still stumbled in his confusion. Maybe it was only some of the wynds that were gone up. The bastard would never burn them all. He turned into the Moss field where he could hear the horses snorting in the semi-darkness. The dawn was just breaking.

When he came to the bottom of the next field, he got the whiff of burning hay. *Dear God,* he prayed silently, *let it be only some of them.* But when he rounded the corner of the hilly field above the glen, he saw that his prayers were not going to be answered. Every wynd was on fire, some of them already reduced to smouldering black circles.

He stood there rooted to the ground in horror. His wonderful golden hay all gone up in smoke. What a bloody waste! That lunatic across the river must be gone off his head. It was a long time since he had been as drastic as this, although things like this had happened before. Jack remembered these same meadows flattened by a herd of cows before they had even been cut and, another time, some sheep dead and dying there after dogs had been set on them. All terrible at the time, but he had got over it. He tried to reason himself into accepting this loss, but despite his best efforts there was a lump of despair in the pit of his stomach. When was all this going to end? He took off his cap and wiped the tears that he felt on his cheeks, uncertain if they were tears of anguish or anger.

"Jack, I know it's terrible, but we'll get over it." Nora, coming up beside him in the darkness, put her arms around him.

"I suppose I'm a foolish old man, Nora, to be crying over hay," he said ruefully.

"You are not, Jack; it's because you were so delighted to have it all saved ready for the barn."

"Well, we'll have a gap in the barn after this."

"Come on down to the rest of them," she said, taking his hand.

"Who's down there?" he asked.

"Peter, Davy, Mom and Uncle Mark," she said. "It was Uncle Mark called us, after waking Davy, who was the nearest."

They could hear Davy holding forth as they approached.

"We should go over and burn him out. If we put up with this, he'll come again."

"You're right," Peter agreed angrily. "We can't take

this lying down. The mad bastard could burn us out."

"Take it easy, lads," Mark intercepted gently. In the half-light he looked like a biblical figure with his long hair and beard and flowing clothes.

"Aisy, is it?" Davy demanded. "How could you take it aisy and look at all that it front of you?"

Jack knew exactly how Davy felt, but Mark was a peaceful soul. They all continued to air different points of view, but he scarcely heard them he was so wrapped up in his inner misery. After a few minutes, he became aware that one voice was silent. Martha was saying nothing. He looked around and saw her face in the grey light that was now filling the meadow. She was oblivious to the voices around her, and her eyes were fastened on Conways'. Her face was rigid with suppressed rage, and it struck Jack then that there was no need for any of them to get even with the Conways, because Martha was going to deal with it, and that when she did there would be no turning back. Something in her expression put a cold finger around his heart.

Silence descended and they continued to stand there until the last wynd smouldered to the ground, as if they could not move until the flames died down. *We are a bit like mourners at a funeral,* Jack thought, *waiting until the last sod goes over the coffin.* Then it was Martha who spoke.

"We are going back up to the house to have a warm breakfast or we'll all get our death of cold standing here." She strode up the field without a backward glance.

They trailed after her. Mark was between Peter and Davy, trying to calm them down, but he was fighting an uphill battle as they were swearing vengeance. Nora and Jack brought up the rear with Nora holding his hand to comfort him. As he walked up the field, he thought of Nellie and felt that in some way she was very close to them this morning.

They were glad to come into the warm kitchen. Martha put on the kettle and laid the table without a word, stirred up the porridge on the Aga and pushed a tray of bacon into the oven. Then she looked at Jack wordlessly, went to the parlour and came down with a bottle wrapped in brown paper. She poured some of the contents into a mug and added sugar and water from the boiling kettle.

"Drink that," she instructed.

He was glad when it scorched down into his stomach and got the blood warming in his veins.

"You needed that," Davy told him. "You looked like a fellow headed for the big brown box until you got that inside your shirt."

"God bless you, Davy, but you're gifted in your choice of words," Jack told him.

"Sit down and have the breakfast," Martha instructed.

When they were all seated around the table, they were silent for a few moments, busy getting warm food inside of them. Then Peter voiced what they were all thinking.

"Well, what are we going to do?" he asked.

"Maybe the proper thing is to report it to the Guards," Mark suggested.

"Waste of time," Davy maintained. "Hours ₍of questioning, measuring and checking times, and by the way, Mark, what time did you notice that we were on fire?"

"About half two I'd say. I was painting and I happened to glance out the window. I couldn't believe what I was seeing down the glen. I might as well have stayed at home for all the good it did. There was nothing to be done."

"No," Jack agreed, "once dry hay gets going there is nothing can stop it, and anyway no cow would touch it after the smoke."

"Conway must have been watching from under some bush across the river having a great laugh at our expense," Peter said bitterly. "We can't let him get away with it."

"We should burn him out," Davy decided.

"But what about Danny and Mrs Conway?" Nora protested. "They would suffer then, and I'd say that they have an awful time with him."

"How do you know?" Peter demanded.

"Well, she looks so sad," Nora told him, "and Danny is always looking after her."

"If he was any good, he'd have that old bastard shot or knifed by now," Peter declared.

"Peter, don't say things like that," Mark protested.

"Nora is right: we can't harm the rest of them."

"So you think that the Guards are the only solution?" Peter asked. "I don't have much faith in doing it that way, because he'll deny everything and we have no proof. They never got him for any of the other stunts he pulled."

The argument went back and forth around the table, with Peter and Davy wanting to take the law into their own hands and Mark and Nora urging restraint. Jack was too tired to argue, and no solution would bring back his fine fields of hay. Martha said nothing, and Jack watched her out of the corner of his eye. She was holding her powder until they all had argued themselves to a standstill. He knew that she had decided on her plan of action down in the meadow as she stared across the river at Conways'.

She rose from the table, and all eyes swung towards her.

"We will do nothing. The time is not right. And don't any of you two do anything stupid," she warned Peter and Davy. "Now it's time to milk the cows." With that she started to clear the breakfast things off the table to growls of protest from Peter and Davy.

"I'll bring the cows," Jack told them, moving out of the kitchen.

The day passed slowly, and Jack was relieved when evening came and he made his weary way home. It seemed like months since he had walked up here last night with a satisfied mind. It would be good to sit by the fire and have a snooze. The hens and ducks were locked up for the night, and he was glad to go into the kitchen and find the fire lighting. Sarah was a great neighbour. It was a wonder she did not stay on to discuss the fire, but she had probably figured that he needed time to himself after the upset. As he lit his pipe for a relaxing smoke, he decided that after a little rest he would go out and do a bit of gardening. It might do him good.

He must have dozed off for a while until he heard a heavy footstep on the path outside. When he saw Matt Conway passing the window, a suppressed anger that had been smouldering since that morning roared through him. He reached back and pulled out his shotgun that he used for shooting rabbits and the odd pheasant from the press beside him. When Matt Conway opened the door, he was looking into the barrel.

"Easy, old man," he growled, showing no semblance of fear. "I'm not going to do you any harm."

"You've done enough harm for one day," Jack told him in a voice trembling with anger. "Get out of here or I'll spatter your brains all over that wall."

"Don't do anything stupid, old man," Conway warned. "If I finish up dead, you'll finish up in jail."

"I'm sorely tempted," Jack told him, "but you're not worth it. Just don't move one inch further into this kitchen. What do you want?"

"I want my meadows back."

"They're not your meadows. Will you ever get that into your thick skull?"

"They're mine by right."

"That they're not," Jack said, "and how come that now all of a sudden you're stepping up the pressure to get them back when you've done nothing with the last eight years?"

"She's of no consequence. She's not a Phelan. It would be no good to get them off her, but the young fellow is back now, another Phelan just like the grandfather before him. I'm going to get them back off him."

"That you're not," Jack told him with determination.

"I can do worse than last night," Conway threatened.

"Two can play that game," Jack told him.

"Some people are better at it, and some of the things I have in mind will make the meadows look like a very cheap price to pay." Conway smiled, and then he was gone, closing the door quietly behind him. Jack felt the blood thumping through his head. *Ease down,* he told himself, *or you'll get a stroke or a heart attack or some other shagging thing.*

Half an hour later when Kate came in, he was still sitting with the gun across his knees.

"Jack, what are you doing with the gun?" she demanded in amazement.

"God, Kate, am I glad to see you," he told her. The very sight of her was a comfort to him. She was the daughter he never had and they understood each other completely. Dark and vivacious as a child, she had grown into an attractive, vibrant woman with a down-to-earth common sense that brought things into perspective. She was just what he needed now.

"I heard about the fire — the whole countryside is talking about it, of course — but what's with the gun?" she asked, taking it off his knees and replacing it in the press.

"Sit down there, Kate, until I tell the whole story."

She drew up a chair beside him and he told her from the very beginning: from the actual saving of the hay and how good he had felt about it, right up to Matt Conway's visit. He filled in all the details because he wanted to get them all clear in his own mind and talking to Kate was almost like talking to himself.

"This could get nasty," she breathed.

"It could indeed," he agreed. "I'll have to tell them below about he coming here and the threats. That'll drive Peter and Davy mad altogether."

"Martha is right, they'll have to be very careful not to get drawn into anything that they can't get out of," Kate said.

"You're right," Jack agreed, "but in another way I'm nearly more nervous of her."

"If Martha moves, she will be deadly, silent, and she won't get caught," Kate told him.

"I know, but I'm still a bit uneasy about her," Jack said.

"Well, don't be," Kate advised. "Martha and I don't

always see eye to eye, but on this occasion I think that she has what it takes. So you stop worrying now, Jack, and after the tea the two of us will go down to Mossgrove, and you can tell them about your caller so that they can keep their ears and eyes open."

"What a way to live," Jack sighed.

"Now, Jack, will you stop worrying," Kate scolded. "It's bad for you, and now that I'm here, I'll check the old ticker and the blood pressure. Wouldn't it suit Matt Conway fine if you died of natural causes?"

"By God, there is no way I'd give him the satisfaction."

"That's more like it now, Jack," Kate told him smiling. "You're the most balanced head we have in Mossgrove, so you must keep going."

As they sat having tea, Jack could feel himself relaxing. Kate always had this effect on him. As district nurse she probably came up against some traumatic situations. *When you deal with birth and death as part of your job, it probably gives you a fairly balanced view of life,* Jack decided.

"How is David?" he asked her.

"Grand," she answered, her face lighting up into a smile. "Himself and Fr Tim have taken the under-age team over to Ross for the final."

"They get on well together," he ventured.

"Do you know something, Jack, they're like brothers. They like the same books, go fishing together and get great satisfaction out of training the teams. Fr Tim is such fun. He makes a great difference to both our lives."

It made him sad to think that such friendship was soon going to get a knock on the head. Kate was continuing, "Fr Tim was dismayed that a farmer would actually burn hay. He has this reverence for the produce of the earth. He thinks that the harvest is the manifestation of 'Give us this day our daily bread'."

"You can tell him from me," Jack told her, "that it's a long time since Matt Conway said the Our Father, and if he does it's his own daily bread he is thinking about, not ours."

CHAPTER SEVEN

K ATE OPENED THE letter with the American stamp
and smiled in delight.

"Rodney Jackson is coming," she told David,
whose dark head was visible above the paper.

"Good," he said vaguely.

"Isn't it great?" she insisted.

"Very," he mumbled

"Very what?" she demanded

"Very interesting," he said.

"What's interesting?" Kate asked.

"Whatever you said," he answered.

"What did I say?" she demanded.

"You have me now," he admitted, lowering the paper
and grinning across at her.

"You're not a morning person," Kate told him, "and
I should have learnt after eight years that at breakfast
I'm talking to myself."

"Let's start again," David told her folding the news-paper and putting it away. "It was something about Rodney Jackson, wasn't it?"

"You got it! Some part of your brain must have been ticking over. He's coming for a few weeks."

"That will give Lizzy and Julia something to keep them occupied," David declared.

"He creates a great stir every time he comes, doesn't he," Kate said with relish, "and it's the last thing that he wants to do."

"Well, he does stand out a bit in the crowd, but I sup-pose with his height it's understandable, and then he doesn't dress like a local farmer."

"And the funny thing is," Kate said, "that he'd love to fit in so well that he wouldn't be noticed."

"Well, tell him this time to put on a pair of welling-tons and a torn jumper and not to shave for a week."

"Could you imagine him?" Kate laughed.

"No," David admitted, "but no matter what he did, he'd never look as if he were born in Kilmeen. You only acquire his look after years of the good life."

"And he sure looks good," Kate said in an affected American drawl.

"And most women in Kilmeen would agree with you," David told her.

"If I weren't so happy with my lot," Kate smiled, "I'd be throwing my hat into the ring too."

"One good man is enough for any woman," David told her, rising from his chair and ruffling her hair as he slipped on his tweed jacket. She reached up her arms and drew his head down and they kissed long and lingeringly.

"A day doesn't begin any better than this." David smiled down at her lovingly.

"You might not be too attentive to conversation in the morning," Kate told him, "but you're all switched on in other departments."

"You smell so good," David told her, burying his face in her hair.

Suddenly the door burst open and Fr Brady shot in waving a letter.

"We're playing Ross in the final on Sunday. . ." and then he stopped short and smiled at them. "Isn't that a great way to begin the day?"

"Nearly as good as morning prayers," David laughed, "but I'd best get down to the school and get the young in off the street before Fr Burke complains again that they are making too much noise."

"Never happy unless he is complaining," Fr Brady assured him.

"I'll see you for training at lunchtime, and were you saying that the final is fixed for Sunday?"

"Oh, that's right," Fr Brady told him.

"That will sort out the men from the boys, as Jack would say," David declared, going out the door and blowing a kiss to Kate over his shoulder.

"Sit down and have a cup of tea with me, Fr Tim," Kate invited him.

"Delighted to," he told her, "but stay where you are and I'll get a cup myself."

"Well, how are things?" she asked as she poured.

"Oh, the usual," he told her, "himself complaining and me trying to turn a deaf ear."

"Nothing changes," she sighed.

"Sometimes I get fed up with it, to be honest," he told her seriously, "and I wonder will I ever be able to stick it."

"Oh my God, I never thought that he was getting under your skin to that extent."

"Well, not all the time," he admitted. "Sometimes there is a clear run and then all hell breaks loose. Maybe it's just that we see the priesthood in a totally different light."

"Thank God for that. No parish could survive two of him," Kate declared as she poured him a second cup of tea. It always amused her the way Fr Tim did everything so fast. It could not be good for him to be always on the go, and she felt sure that it was only when he was fishing that he came to a standstill. He was full of compressed energy, and she knew from experience that he moved first and asked questions afterwards. But for now he seemed to be putting thought into what he was about to say.

"Well, what is it?" she prompted him. "You seem to have something stuck in your craw, as Jack would say."

"Kate, would you give me a straight answer to something that's bothering me?" he asked.

"Try me," Kate told him, "and I'll do my best."

"How am I shaping up as a priest?" he asked. "Sometimes I have huge doubts about my suitability for this business."

Kate looked at him in amazement.

"You're the best," she told him. "You're what it's all about, and that's not alone my opinion but the opinion of most people in the parish, especially the young ones."

"Sometimes I think that I'm a bit of a fraud," he said grimly. "I preach the love of God to people, but there are times when I question if he is even there."

"Don't we all?" Kate assured him. "But despite that we still keep going, and then one day something happens and you know that he is right there in the heart of everything. When I sit by the deathbeds of old country people who have lived close to the earth and God all their lives, I feel Him with them. Their simple faith confirms me in mine."

"I know what you mean," Fr Tim agreed slowly. "Death is a sobering moment, when all the masks slip away and you see reality. Some of these old country people are amazing."

"Not all of them, mind you," Kate smiled. "Probably only the ones who found their own inner harmony. I was with my mother when she died, and she slipped away as quietly as she had lived."

"'As a man lives, so shall he die,'" Fr Tim quoted to himself.

"I suppose," Kate continued, "if we haven't found God in our daily round, nothing is going to change in death."

"He is very important to you, isn't He?" Fr Tim asked.

"I don't often sit down and analyse things like we're doing now, but in my job I feel His power when I watch people die and, at the other end of the scale, when I help deliver a baby."

"Whenever I meet you after you've delivered a baby, there is a special glow about you," Fr Tim smiled.

"It's a miracle every time," she told him.

They sat in silence for a while.

"It must be very hard not to have one of your own," he said gently.

"Very," she told him grimly.

"You never mention it."

"Maybe I'm afraid that if I start talking I'll never stop. I don't want it to become an obsession with me because in many ways I have so much. David and I are very happy together and I know that he would love a child, but because he knows that I feel the same way, we try not to let it become a mountain in our lives. We have almost come to the stage now where neither of us brings it up in case of upsetting the other, and that's not right either."

"Understandable though."

"Still, it's good to discuss it occasionally, and strangely enough Jack and myself sometimes talk about it."

"You're very fond of Jack," Fr Tim smiled.

"He's been the backbone of my life, always there through every storm that blew through Mossgrove," she said thoughtfully.

"The last one shook him up quite a bit," Fr Tim said.

"It did indeed," Kate sighed. "His hay would be sacred in Jack's eyes, and to see it being burned was almost like scorching himself."

"Hard to understand Conway," Fr Tim said.

"What was it St Paul said: 'Understand it even though it's beyond all understanding.' "

"Never knew that you were a biblical scholar."

"Funny the way you remember certain little bits," Kate told him. "Oh, and by the way, I almost forgot to tell you that Rodney Jackson is coming soon."

"The dashing American rides into town," Fr Tim smiled. "No Mrs Jackson yet?"

"Not yet," Kate told him, "but if he is on the look-out, there would be no shortage of contenders around here."

"He would probably fancy an Irish wife," Fr Tim suggested.

"Well, he has decided that everything else Irish is to his satisfaction anyway."

"You must know him pretty well at this stage since he always stays here with you," Fr Tim said.

"What you see is what you get. Direct, generous and decisive, wielding huge power in his business world, and yet very unassuming and very anxious to do everything that's good for Kilmeen on account of the family connection here."

"He has made a big difference to this place," Fr Tim remarked.

"Getting the old Jackson house for the school was wonderful for David, and he has never looked back. And, of course, what Rodney has done for Mark is fantastic. Now Rodney is organising this exhibition in New York and Mark is going over for it."

"He must be worth a fortune."

"I'd say so," Kate said, "but he keeps a very low tone about it. He thinks that we Irish are very special, so much so that he almost tiptoes around local sensibilities in case he'd upset anyone."

"God help him," Fr Tim declared, "he's in for a rude awakening some day."

"Oh, you of little faith," Kate smiled. "You must have got out of the wrong side of the bed this morning."

"Something like that," he admitted, rising from the chair, "but do you know what, Kate? I'm the better for talking to you. You always straighten me up and face me in the right direction when I find myself going astray."

"A signpost," Kate told him laughing. "Maybe I should stand up at the village corner and point people in the right direction."

After Fr Tim had gone, she sat thinking about him. She was extremely fond of him and sometimes she worried that he had become too big a part of her life. He seemed to have slipped into Ned's shoes, and she depended on him to discuss and tease out things with her. But whereas Ned had been tranquil and calming, Fr Tim, although he had the same deep sensitivity as Ned, was full of restless energy. It was just as well that she loved David deeply and had done so since she was a teenager, because it would be very easy to be carried away by the vibrancy and excitement of Fr Tim. The fact that he was totally unaware of his appeal made him more appealing, and maybe the fact that he had a collar around his neck marking him as unavailable added to that.

As there was still about half an hour before the dispensary opened, Kate walked out into the garden. She liked to stroll around the garden in the morning and see how everything had survived the night, and she never failed to be delighted at the little changes each day brought. Now she saw that one of her mother's old roses, which she had transplanted with care from Mossgrove, was turning from a bud into bloom. Its deep rich aroma more than compensated for its lack of showmanship. Kate always thought of it as a quiet rose. It could almost go unnoticed as you walked around the garden, but once you had passed, it reached after you and enveloped you in veils of fragrance, and then you returned, apologetic for overlooking it in the first place. Since she had moved in here she had tended this garden with loving care and turned it into her haven of delight. She came out here to be healed when she returned home after handling sad cases on her rounds. In the early days of her marriage, she had visualised a pram under the tree at the end of the garden.

She thought of the impending visit of Rodney Jackson and his big plans for Mark's exhibition. It gave them all something to look forward to, which was a great thing after the upheaval of the hay burning. It was wonderful the way he loved this place and came as often as he could. Maybe Fr Tim was right and that he might meet a local girl. *Pity that Nora is too young,* Kate thought. *Wouldn't she just love flitting back and forth on his trips with him?* Kate smiled to herself. She had better watch herself or she'd turn into a second Julia or Lizzy.

CHAPTER EIGHT

F R TIM BRADY put his back to the altar and looked down at the congregation. He did not normally say the second mass. Fr Burke, the parish priest, always kept that mass for himself. The PP called the first mass the creamery mass, bluntly saying that the great unwashed went to it, because the men who brought the milk to the creamery came to it on their way home. But today he was confined to his bed with a summer bug and had Lizzy running up and down the stairs fetching and carrying.

The church was full but not as packed as it had been at the first mass. In winter the biggest crowd was at second mass, but farming people could not afford to lie in bed on a summer's morning. But whichever mass they went to, it amused him the way people always went to their own place. *We are creatures of habit*, he thought.

Martha Phelan sat impassively four rows from the front, beautiful, remote and controlled. One could never be sure what was going on behind that glacial facade. Beside her sat sunny-faced Nora. It was hard to think that they were mother and daughter, but Peter at the back of the church was surely his mother's son. He was dynamite on the field and there was no beating him once he got going. The same would apply to his mother. *I wouldn't like to cross her*, Tim thought.

Across the aisle sat the Conways. Big burly Matt always reminded him of a Hereford bull, with the personality to match. Biddy Conway looked as if she were apologetic for the space she was taking up. Poor woman. What a miserable life she had. If Danny got half a chance he had the makings of a grand lad, but the odds were stacked against him.

Sarah Jones was a few seats behind the Conways. She was a pleasant woman who kept her mind to herself and only spoke up when things were seriously out of step. Across the aisle from her were Kate and David, a smashing couple. Kate was like a ray of sunshine in her yellow dress.

"My dear brethren," he began, "today we are going to go back to the beginning. To the first prayer that Our Lord gave to His disciples. He told them, 'This is how you pray . . . Our Father who art in heaven, hallowed be thy name, thy kingdom come, thy will be done on earth as it is in heaven. Give give us this day our daily bread. . .'," and he stopped for a few moments. "It's with this part of the Our Father we will concern our-selves today. 'Give us this day our daily bread.' We are asking the Lord to bless us with the fruits of the earth. It is a wonderful petition, and the Lord in his generos-ity grants it abundantly. The earth is generous and we depend on it for our daily bread. In this farming com-munity, we are very aware of that. At the moment we are in the midst of the haymaking season, the hay that will feed our cattle who provide us with milk and the milk cheque with which people buy the necessities of life in this community. We must treasure and respect the fruits of the earth. They are not ours, and we must never destroy them because that is going against the laws of nature. They are the gifts of God and the answer to our request, 'Give us this day our daily bread.'"

There was absolute silence in the church. He con-tinued, "The next line of the Lord's Prayer says, 'and forgive us our trespasses as we forgive those who tres-pass against us'. This is surely a testing part of this prayer. But we must leave old hurts behind. So let us go forth in peace to love God, and that means loving our neighbour as well. In the name of the Father and of the Son and of the Holy Ghost, Amen."

After the final prayers he returned to the sacristy with the altar boys. He was just removing his surplice when the door crashed open and Matt Conway burst in roaring, "If you think that you can read me off the altar, you half-baked priest, and get away with it, you have something else coming to you."

Before Fr Tim had time to recover, he was caught by the bunched up surplice, lifted off the floor and thrown back into a corner full of tall brass candlesticks that clattered in all directions. He recovered himself quickly and wondered if he should try to placate the man or sort him out at his own game. The choice was not his, however, as Conway was coming at him again with his head down. The Lord had said turn the other cheek, but in this case it could be reduced to pulp, and maybe the Lord did not have a little lightweight boxing experience. Swinging out a right uppercut, he landed Matt Conway into a bunch of altar boys. He had forgotten all about the altar boys, who were watching in open-mouthed amazement. *My God, what stories they will make out of this!* Before Conway got to his feet, Tim whipped open the door and ordered the astonished boys, "Out."

He was glad they were gone when Conway, regaining his feet, spat out, "I'll sort you out, yourself and that Kate Phelan, playing around under that fool of a husband's nose. Is that barren old bitch hoping that you'll produce the child that she's waiting for?"

All thoughts of turning the other cheek were banished and he was back in the ring with all the old skills. Matt Conway did not know what hit him. He had never been beaten in a fight, but then he had never come up against a boxer. It was like trying to hit a flying object, and the punches came at him from where he least expected. Finally he backed to the door, but before he disappeared, he left his threat: "This will cost you the collar, you cur."

When he was gone Tim collapsed into the nearest chair. He had forgotten the pleasures of boxing and had got immense satisfaction from getting the better of Conway. He had always felt sorry for Biddy, especially since he found out about Conway throwing her down the stairs. Then there was the sorry story of Mary and Kitty. Oh yes, he had a lot of scores to settle with Conway. But was this the way a priest should act? Oh boy, was he in trouble now. Big trouble! It was probably unheard of in any parish for the curate to beat up a parishioner, no matter what the reason. He closed his eyes and groaned aloud, "Oh God, I'm supposed to be preaching and practising love your neighbour. Oh Brady, you've really torn it this time."

He sat for a long time with his face in his hands, trying to figure out where he was going to go from here. Burke would be down on him like a ton of bricks. He was always complaining about too much time at games and too much time fishing. There was no end to what was wrong. *Now, you fool,* he thought, *you've played right into his hands. He'll be delighted to fill the bishop in and get you out of here. You'll probably finish up in the back of nowhere, if you don't finish up nowhere at all.* What were the steps to being thrown out? He had had no reason to find out before but, by God, he had good reason now. Maybe he should spare them the trouble and go anyway.

Suddenly he remembered that the candles were still lighting out on the altar because he had rushed the altar boys off before they had time to finish their jobs. He went out into the silent church and put them out. The church had the warmth of the recent occupancy of many people. He had grown to love this church during his ten years here, especially the richly coloured stained-glass windows. When the sun poured through them, it turned the place into a rainbow. He came back into the sacristy and locked the door.

He was loth to leave the sacristy, not quite sure of what lay outside. How could he face people on the street and how would they react? It was undoubtedly the talk of the village by now and would be all over the parish in a matter of hours. Oh boy, had he blown it.

Then another more frightening thought struck him, what Conway had said about himself and Kate. Could people really be talking about them? Whatever about belting Conway, if there was talk about Kate and himself, he was really in trouble. A step in that direction and they crucified you altogether! He didn't know whether he was coming or going. What did he really feel about Kate? He thought she was like the sister he never had, but then what did he know about that? He had never had a sister, and maybe what he felt for Kate was more than that. He loved being with her and they had great fun together and he had never thought very much about it, but maybe that was not right either. His head was so addled he did not know what to think.

Suddenly there was a knock on the side door of the sacristy. *This is it*, he thought. *Burke is after hearing it and he wants me up*. He remained sitting, reluctant to open the door.

"Come in," he called, and to his amazement Davy Shine breezed in.

"Father, I heard you beat the pulp out of Conway. That was well coming to him. Coming to him with years," Davy proclaimed with relish. "Whatever good you have done in this parish up to now, and you've done a lot of good with the teams and everything, it's nothing compared to this. This beats all! I think you should start a boxing club."

Tim looked at Davy Shine in disbelief, and in the face of his lighthearted assessment, the whole situation seemed less threatening. His sense of trauma cracked and he burst out laughing.

"Davy, you're incredible," he said.

"Whatever that's supposed to mean I'm not sure, but we're all waiting for you up in the field for the match. How could you forget about the final? Come on and don't be keeping us all waiting."

"By God, Davy, you saved my sanity," Tim said.

"I hope I'll save a few goals now and keep the pressure off Danny," Davy told him.

They walked up to the field together and the few people they met along the street were as friendly as usual. Maybe the people might have no problem with what happened, but unfortunately they did not have the final say. In the field all the lads were raring to go, and once the match started he got so caught up in the excitement he almost forgot his troubles. When Kilmeen scored the winning point in the last few minutes, there was general elation.

Afterwards Peter came over to him.

"You played a blinder this morning on the altar," he said.

"Might have played myself off it," Fr Tim said ruefully.

"It was the first sermon I ever heard that applied to Kilmeen. I'm tired of hearing about Cana and these places. We don't live there, we live here, and we want sermons about how to live here."

"Everyone might not agree with you," Fr Tim told him.

"I heard that," Peter smiled, "and you beat down the opposition."

"Not a very priestly thing to do. There'll be repercussions without a doubt."

As he was leaving the field, David Twomey caught up with him.

"Well, how's the champ?" he greeted Tim, his dark attractive face full of amusement.

"I'd say that the champ is in the height of trouble," Tim told him.

"Could be a bit sticky for a while, but it should be all right."

"I'm not so sure. Fr Burke will annihilate me. I'm

bound to be shifted if I'm not kicked out all together."

"Tim, don't lose your sense of proportion. You only gave the man a few belts, you didn't kill him, for God's sake," David protested, "and if anyone had it coming he had. He's been knocking people about all his life. He was such a bloody bear that nobody could get the better of him."

"No strategy or technique," Tim analysed; "would never do in the ring."

"We must start a boxing club," David said enthusiastically.

"Oh, for God's sake, not you, too."

"Who else got the brainwave?" he asked.

"Davy Shine," Tim answered.

"Good man, Davy Shine. There is no substitute for running with the ball when you get it."

"I could be running faster than I expected."

"Come on down with me for the tea," David invited. "You're not fit company for yourself."

"That's more of the problem," Tim told him.

"How do you mean?"

"I'll tell you when we get down to Kate," he said.

They were sitting around the table in Kate's kitchen with garden fragrances floating in the open door and window. Any other day Tim would have enjoyed looking out into the garden, but now his mind was in turmoil.

"This is so embarrassing," he told them, "but I had better fill you in."

107

"Fr Tim, you're actually blushing. What's going on with you?" Kate asked.

"It's a case of what's going on between the two of us is the problem," he told her.

"What!"

"There is no easy way of putting this," he told her. "Matt Conway suggests that you and I have something going on between us on the quiet."

An amused grin spread over Kate's face.

"God, Fr Tim, I'm flattered that a handsome lad like you would set his cap at an old married lady like me."

"It's no joke, Kate," he warned. "If this gets out, I'm in more trouble."

"Tim, you've got all this out of perspective. Matt Conway is capable of saying anything," David told him, "and nobody would take any notice of him."

"I don't know whether I'm coming or going after this morning," Tim admitted.

"I'll check out the rumour with Sarah," Kate told him, "just to put your mind at rest. She always know what's going on, and in the mean while don't be looking for trouble. It might all blow over. But if you had told me about giving that sermon, I'd have told you not to."

"There are things, Kate, that are just wrong no matter what way you look at it, and burning good hay is one of them. I was not going to let it pass," he said.

"Better for you if you had," she told him.

"Well, Kate, he didn't," David interjected, "and I

think that he was right. Sometimes the Church has to grasp the nettle. Now let's drop this stupid subject and discuss the match. We won today. Let's enjoy the victory, not anticipate a storm that might never come."

When Tim opened his front door later, there was a note on the mat from Fr Burke instructing him to be up at the presbytery on Wednesday morning after mass. The storm was not going to blow over; it was about to reach gale force. But the PP was going to keep him in suspense for two days.

CHAPTER NINE

WHEN THE DINNER was over and she had tidied away, Martha looked around with satisfaction. She liked a spotless kitchen with everything in its place. Untidy people annoyed her, and she had long ago decided that those who lived in confusion usually finished up confused. When she thought of confusion a picture of Mark's studio always came to mind, because there was no denying but that he lived in a muddle. How he produced anything out of that jumble was beyond belief. Her mother never interfered with him, but then Agnes was easygoing and it did not seem to bother her; and she was so proud of him now that he was doing well.

It was strange the way Rodney Jackson had come back into their lives after all those years. Since those childhood visits to his aunts, they had not seen him again until eight years ago. When he had come then, this extremely tall, good-looking American had created quite a stir in Kilmeen, and since then he had returned regularly, much to the interest of the female population of the village.

This Rodney Jackson had a strange idea that Mark was something special, and the price he had paid Mark for all those pictures that were hanging in David Twomey's school was amazing. But then, the Miss Jacksons had been into that kind of thing as well. They had looked after Mark well when they were alive, and even now that they were dead he was still benefiting. Mark had always got the good end of the stick!

As children she and Mark had never been close and this gap had widened in recent years. Ned and himself had been close friends, and Kate and himself had been buddies for years. As children Peter and Nora had loved him because he was almost of their world, and when his pictures were hung in their school and impressed all their friends, they hero-worshipped him. If ever Martha criticised Mark, they all sprang to his defence. It annoyed her intensely the way that he was inevitably on the opposite side to her whenever there was a conflict of opinions in Mossgrove.

She was now about to walk back to her old home to discuss with Mark and Agnes whether she could have the use of their land to supplement the loss of the river meadow hay. Agnes and Mark wouldn't mind, but she disliked being in the position of having to ask. She had expected that they might have offered, but it probably had never crossed their minds. She knew that they had not sold off the meadows as yet this year, so she was going to pay them whatever they had earned last year. She was not coming to them cap in hand, as Jack would term it.

It was such a lovely day that she decided to take the short cut through the fields instead of going around by the longer road. The only people using this short cut were themselves and the Shines, but the path was well worn as Nora and Peter were always back and forth to Mark and Agnes. As she walked along the hilly field behind the house, she saw Matt Conway leaning on his stake over Yalla Hole, looking across. The sight of him and the black circles in the meadow rekindled her anger. So he thought that she was of no consequence and that she did not rate very much because she was a woman and not a Phelan? Even though it had prevented him from making a nusiance of himself during the last eight years, his reasoning irked her. He might discover that she was of more consequence than he thought.

It had surprised her greatly that Fr Brady had brought up the subject of the hay burning at mass on Sunday. She would not have thought that he had the courage. He was too good-looking for his own good, but apparently there was more to him than a handsome exterior. When Lizzie had passed that smart remark behind her back in the post office, she had ignored her, but it was no wonder that there were rumours going around about himself and Kate. If he had been an over-weight, plain-looking man like Fr Burke, there would have been no gossip. She knew Kate well enough to know that Kate would not dream of having a fling on the side. Besides, she had been long enough setting her cap at David Twomey before they finally got things sorted out. It just went to show that people could get any kind of a rumour going. Still, it amused her that do-gooding Kate could be the victim of wagging tongues.

She followed the path at the bottom of the field down into the small wood overlooking the river. The trees were like huge umbrellas screening out the sun, and she was glad to walk along in the cool green shadows. She had often played here as a child, solitary games with imaginary people who lived under the trees. As a teenager this had been her refuge when she had found it difficult to be one of the crowd. If Mark and herself were different from each other, they were also different from other people. But whereas Mark was tolerant of people, she, for the most part, found them slightly irritating. To go her own way and do her own thing had always been her choice.

She might never have got married if Ned had not come to the house most nights with Mark, and slowly she had found herself looking forward to seeing him. Once she had decided that Ned was the one she wanted, she went about achieving her aim with single-minded determination.

They had been very happy together. Ned had never opposed her because when he did she made life so uncomfortable that he soon fell into line. Although her father had died when she was young, she had seen him getting his own way and Agnes agreeing for the sake of a quiet life. She had been determined that she would be the one in control if she ever got married.

Leaving the river behind, she climbed up the steep path using the tree trunks as hand rails. How quiet it was in here with only the birds and the occasional rustle in the undergrowth. She came out of the wood into the field below her old home, and as she followed the winding path she thought over what she was going to say to her mother and Mark.

The house was an extraordinary colour. How Agnes could have let Mark put that amazing yellow on the house and that crazy red on the door she could never understand.

Agnes opened the door with a welcoming smile on her face. When Martha thought about it, which was seldom, she wondered how a pretty, small-boned little person like Agnes could be the mother of herself and Mark. She had once heard old Molly Conway say that "all the oddness came from the Lehanes". That old lady had been a bad-minded cow!

"Martha, it's great to see you; you seldom call by at this time of day," Agnes greeted her.

"I have a reason," Martha told her. "Is Mark here?"

"He's out in the back painting. I don't like to disturb

him when he's stuck into something," Agnes said gently.

"Won't do him any harm," Martha told her, going to the back door and out into the garden.

Martha could just see Mark's back through the high flowers down at the bottom of the garden. She wound her way down through Agnes' idea of a garden towards him. *What a mix up,* she thought as she viewed the potato stalks, cabbage, rhubarb and flowers all growing through each other. *How can anyone tolerate a garden like this?* Her father had had such law and order here in his day, but her mother had let it go higgley-piggley and all over the place.

She watched Mark for a little while. He was completely engrossed in what he was doing and had not heard her coming. On the canvas a butterfly was taking shape, and then she noticed that there was one flitting around a bush just in front of him. How could he stand here so still, just watching a butterfly?

"Mark," she said sharply, "I want to talk to you and mother about something."

He remained standing with his back to her, and she could sense his annoyance at the interruption, but when he turned towards her, his face was expressionless.

"Butterflies are so delicate," he told her mildly, laying his brush and palette on the low hedge. "We'll go in and have a cup of tea together."

"I have no time for tea," she told him.

"Well, I have," he said evenly, following her up the garden.

Agnes had the cups on the table and was making the tea as they came into the kitchen. *This kitchen has become more cluttered over the years,* Martha thought as she viewed her mother's sewing machine in the corner with half-finished work draped over it, knitting needles stuck in a ball of wool on the windowsill and sketches finished and unfinished propped up in different corners.

"This place could do with a good tidying," she told them.

"Don't even think about it," Mark smiled. "Agnes and I know where to lay our hands on everything."

"You're two of a kind," she told them.

"That's why we live in such harmony," Mark told her.

"Nothing allowed to interfere with your creative talent, you mean," Martha told him.

"The creative muse is disturbed by discord," Mark smiled, "so we don't upset each other."

"Aren't you so lucky that you can keep it all outside the door. Some of us don't have that choice."

"Well, I suppose with neighbours like the Conways it isn't that easy," Mark agreed.

"It's as a result of them that I'm here," Martha told him.

Agnes, having poured the tea, had put the teapot back by the fire and joined them at the table.

"You know that Mark and I will do anything we can to help," she told Martha, handing around a plate of scones.

117

"If that's the case, why have you not offered the meadows here to us?" Martha demanded.

"But we have. . ." Mark began and stopped at a warning glance from Agnes, but Martha had seen the exchange of looks and cut in.

"How do you mean, you have?"

"Well, Peter was here after the fire and we told him," Mark said decidedly.

"You did what?" Martha demanded.

"Oh, for goodness sake, Martha! Peter was here that night and, of course, we offered him the meadows."

"But that decision is not Peter's to make," Martha told him.

"Don't be ridiculous, what decision was there? We have uncut meadows and you need hay, so there was no decision involved, just plain common sense," Mark said.

"You should not have discussed this with Peter behind my back. He is not in charge of Mossgrove, and I'm having problems enough with him without you two making it worse."

"Did you ever think, Martha, that you might be making a problem out of nothing?" Mark asked her.

"It's none of your business. I will pay you for the meadows, the same as you got from the Nolans last year."

"You will not," Agnes put in firmly. "We don't need the money. Family is family, and there is no way that Mark and I would charge you and Peter for the use of land that will probably be his anyway."

"How do you mean, his anyway?" Martha exclaimed. "Are you going to hand this land over to Peter?"

"More than likely, unless I get a sudden urge in my declining years and take unto myself a wife, which I don't plan to do," Mark smiled.

"So you would give the land to my son and not to me?" Martha demanded.

"We'll see," Agnes put in quietly, "and anyway, it's nothing that's going to be done today or tomorrow."

"Well, when it is being done, I think that you would do well to remember that a daughter and sister is closer than a grandson or a nephew," she told them.

"We will," Agnes agreed, but she knew that her mother was just placating her for the moment.

"Cutting the meadows here is going to be a lot of extra work," Mark said.

"There are enough of them there to do it," she asserted.

"Well, you know that Jack will insist on doing all the cutting," Mark told her, "and he really is pushing on a bit for that."

"Jack does as Jack wants," she told him, "and that's it."

"If there was a tractor on the farm," Mark suggested, "he would hand over a lot of the work to Peter and Davy, and if you are working the two places, they would really need one."

"And, of course," she said acidly, "Peter has not been talking to you about it."

"Well, he did mention it, and I must say that I agree with him," Mark admitted.

"Needless to mention you agree with him! But then it's not going to cost you anything to agree with him, is it?"

"I'd be glad to help," he told her.

"Keep out of my family," she warned him.

"But is it only the cost that's the problem?" Mark persisted.

"Well, of course, it's only the cost," she told him in an annoyed voice.

"But, Martha, you're not short of a bob," he said.

"Well, if I'm not, I've some other use for it," she retorted.

"Like what?" he persisted.

"You'll find out in due course."

"Interesting," he smiled benignly. "You are always interesting, Martha."

"And I wonder where Peter brings it from?" she snapped.

As she walked home across the fields, she thought back over the conversation. Peter getting her home farm without any consultation with her was a bit high-handed of Mark and Agnes, and she knew by the way they reacted that the decision had already been made. It was a small farm compared to Mossgrove, but it was very good land that had never been properly farmed since her father died. Mark didn't have a clue about farming! If Peter put his mind to it, there was a good living there. It was a disquieting thought.

Just as she turned in the last gap for home, a movement down by the wood caught her eye. A man was walking along in the shadow of the trees. He must have come out of the wood, which meant that he had been just below her path, hidden behind the trees in the undergrowth. As he turned to cross over the ditch, he looked in her direction. It was Matt Conway.

CHAPTER TEN

TIM BRADY HAD never intended to be a priest. One of a family of five boys, he enjoyed dancing, football and girls. He and his brothers helped out after school in the family pub where they argued and fought over hours on and off, arguments usually settled by their mother, who was an expert on calming troubled waters. Being the youngest, he was constantly accused of getting special treatment as his mother's pet. His father was a quiet man who opted for leaving the decisions to his wife, and it was only when things tended to get out of hand that he was called in to voice his opinion. As he generally backed up his wife, the boys had discovered early in life that it was their mother who had to be convinced if they wanted to do anything that needed parental consent.

One night, the year Tim was seventeen, she had gathered them all together into the kitchen behind the pub and told them that she had bad news. Nothing could have prepared them for the shock: she had been diagnosed as having cancer, with only months to live. Their world crashed in around them. There followed months of black despair with occasional rays of hope that were quickly obliterated by deeper despair. Finally it was all over and they moved around the house like shadows in a morgue. For Tim it was a torturous time. His mother had been the glue that had held them all together. Now he was cut adrift in a world that had no centre, as if he had been hurled up into the air and had splintered into many fragments that would not come back together again. During all the trauma, his father had remained silent and bewildered. Sometimes Tim would come on him staring into space, but as soon as he became aware of Tim's presence he would try to pull himself together. Every morning his father crept quietly out of the house for early mass and every night he knelt to say his rosary. Tim watched him and felt that he was beginning to cope because he had access to a spiritual seam that Tim could not understand.

"Boy, when the world is a black pool, you've got to look up or else you'll drown," he told Tim.

If in later years Tim ever questioned himself as to why he had become a priest, and he had often had reason to question himself, he knew that it had something to do with his mother's death. It had turned him into a different person. At the seminary he had often clashed with the powers in charge. One dean had told him, "Brady, you will always be on the edge of trouble." But despite everything he had come through, though he still asked himself at times if he was the right man in the right place. He had found it very difficult to come to terms with the fact that being a priest set you apart from the ordinary people. It was difficult to understand how it happened, but once you were ordained, you were different. People assumed that you were in some way holier and better than them. It might suit some to be on a pedestal, but not him. He had often found it a lonely, frightening place.

The Wednesday morning after his "hay sermon", he thought back over his life since ordination and wondered if he was ever meant to fit into the priestly strait-jacket. Burke was designed for the job; he loved the power and the respect his collar earned him and listening to himself pontificating off the altar every Sunday. Tim constantly found himself unsure of how he should be handling the problems that were thrust upon him as part of his parochial duties. Sometimes he felt that no one man could have the wisdom to be what a really good priest should be, but he did the best he could and often prayed to his mother for guidance. He thought of Kate's opinion that he should not have given the "hay sermon". She was probably right, but then if you were hidebound by too many rules and regulations, you lost your natural instinct.

As he was about to leave the house to say mass, the phone rang and it was Kate.

"I had a chat with Sarah Jones, and the rumour about us is going around, though not widely, but Lizzy is in on it so Fr Burke will know."

"I'm for the high jump this morning after mass, and it's best to know in advance if he has a joker up his sleeve."

"Well, he has that joker anyway and he might have a few more, knowing him," Kate warned, "but whatever you do, don't lose your cool and tear into him, because then he'll be laughing all the way to the bishop."

"I could be going down that road anyway," he said ruefully.

"If you can get it sorted out with him, he will have no reason to go to the bishop," Kate advised.

"Time will tell."

"David thinks that it's much ado about nothing," Kate comforted him.

"I hope he's right."

As he picked up his keys, he glanced around his small hallway with its flagged floor and thought that he would hate to leave this old house into which he had accumulated all his books and bits and pieces over the years. There was something about the essence of this little house that soothed him as soon as he opened the front door. It had a comforting spirit. His father had given him some surplus furniture from the old home when one of his brothers got married. It felt good to have his mother's special pieces around him. Some of the village women thought that he should have a housekeeper, but he liked having the freedom of the house to himself and he enjoyed cooking. When he had moved into the house, every room was painted magnolia, but he had brightened the whole place up with vivid colours. Mark had given him some wonderful pictures and over the years he had got endless pleasure from them. *At least,* he thought, *I can take them with me.*

When he came on to the altar to say the mass, there were the usual few people scattered around the church. He liked the weekday mass. There was something calm and unhurried about it, and he felt, too, that the people who came were there because they wanted to be, though it was probably true that for some of them it was more a habit than anything else. But then who was he to judge? Sarah Jones was there most mornings, having cycled in the few miles. There was a great serenity about her and he felt that she had an unshakeable faith. *I wish that I had her confidence,* he thought. His father had it as well. Was it going to disappear with their generation? But then he doubted that the PP had it. If he had he would have been a kinder man.

After mass Tim walked down the street to his own house and had a quick breakfast. The time on his summons was 10am, so he had best not be late. As he walked in around the back of the church to the parochial house, he envied the birds singing happily on the trees. It was such a lovely morning that he felt cheated to have it blighted by the encounter ahead. He looked up at the fine old trees that lined the avenue into the house and smiled to remember the row when Fr Burke got a notion of cutting them down a few years ago and Kate and David had opposed him.

He lifted the heavy black knocker and could hear the loud clang echoing back the long hallway. After some time when nothing happened, he was just about to lift it again when he heard bolts being pulled and Lizzy's beaky nose peered around the edge of the door. It always annoyed him the way she never opened the door back properly, almost as if she were expecting an attack or to find someone unpleasant on the doorstep. When she saw him it was as if her suspicions were confirmed, and she withdrew slightly with a look of disapproval.

"He's expecting me," he told her, suppressing an impulse to push the door open wide and stride past her.

"I'll see," she sniffed and disappeared. He pushed in the door and walked into the drab brown hallway.

What a depressing hole. It had not got a lick of paint since he had come to the parish, and that was probably because Fr Burke never even noticed it. Perhaps he wanted to portray the image of self-denial and austerity. As Lizzy, thin and drably dressed in tight black clothes, came back into the hall, Tim thought that she blended into it.

"Fr Burke will see you now," she told him, stabbing a purple finger to a door back the hallway.

Fr Burke was a large man who had obviously never denied himself anything at the table. Sitting behind an enormous desk, his recent summer bug had not paled his heavy red face that swept upwards into a glistening bald head edged around with white bristle cut to the bone. As Tim looked at him, he remembered his mother's remark about anybody she considered to be powerfully strong, that "they were fit to plough". Fr Burke fitted the bill.

He continued to write when Tim came in, and the only acknowledgement of his presence was a thick finger pointed at an isolated chair in the middle of the room. *You're being cut down to size, Brady boy,* he told himself. *Burke is really going to enjoy this and he has the stage set for the performance.* He sat on the hard bentwood chair that creaked in protest. Then there was complete silence in the room but for the scratching of Fr Burke's pen. *This silent treatment is to unnerve me,* Tim thought, *so I had better not fall into that trap.* He tried to force his mind back to the mass that morning, but it was difficult to prevent the tension from gripping him.

"Well?" Fr Burke barked.

Tim felt like saying, "Well what?" but knew that it was better to try to keep things as pleasant as possible.

"You sent for me, Father," he said.

"And did that surprise you?" Fr Burke demanded, laying down his pen and settling him with a steely glare.

Now will I start playing his game of dodging around the

issue or go straight to the point? Tim decided on a middle course.

"Maybe not," he said.

"So you have some realisation of what you have done?"

"I suppose it all depends on the way you look at it," he ventured.

"Well, there is only one way to look at it and that's the right way. You beat up a parishioner when he came to voice an opinion and. . ."

"He came to do more than that, I'm afraid," Tim interrupted. "He charged into the sacristy and attacked me first."

"Well, that's not the way I heard it," Fr Burke said heavily.

"Depends on who you believe," Tim said, feeling that he had a right to defend his corner, "and the altar boys saw what happened."

"We won't be dragging the altar boys into this mess. They have been scandalised enough already," Fr Burke told him. "Now, even if the parishioner arrived in the sacristy in an excited state, it was your duty as a priest to calm him down, not to beat him out the door unheard."

"I don't think that he came for a reasonable discussion," Tim said, "and if I had not defended myself, I would have finished up in a pretty battered condition."

"Better you than the parishioner."

"Well, maybe," Tim agreed.

"Now the cause of this argument was the subject of your sermon, which was ill-advised to say the least of it."

"I don't agree with burning the produce of the earth."

"Nobody does, but when the produce in question comes from fields that are the subject of a deep-rooted feud in the parish, you should have kept your mouth shut."

"Maybe in retrospect it might have been better," Tim agreed.

"Much better," Fr Burke confirmed, beginning to look less confrontational and pleased with the way things were going.

Tim began to relax, thinking that maybe they might be able to sort things out.

"So you will go to that parishioner and apologise," Fr Burke told him.

He was just about to open his mouth to protest when his father's advice in a similar situation came back to him: *No skin off your nose, my lad, and a meal of humble pie is very good for the spirit.*

"Very well," he agreed and almost smiled at the surprise on Burke's face, who had been beginning to look like the proverbial cat with the saucer of cream. His next shot was direct, no beating about the bush.

"What's this about yourself and Kate Twomey?" he demanded.

"Gossip," Tim told him.

"A priest cannot afford to be the subject of parish gossip."

"When there is no truth in the gossip, it burns itself out," Tim asserted.

"By then it will have done a certain amount of damage by breaking people's trust and respect for their priest."

"If someone decides to start a malicious rumour, there is very little that can be done."

"There is, by not giving any grounds for talk in the first place," Fr Burke pronounced.

"So what do you suggest?" Tim asked.

"No more visiting Kate and David Twomey."

"But they're my friends," Tim protested.

"Well, that's the source of the gossip, and if you want to nip it, that's what you have to do," Fr Burke told him.

Tim was taken aback. David and Kate were part of the reason that he liked Kilmeen. David and himself got much enjoyment out of training the teams and spent many pleasant hours fishing together, and it was great to be able to pop in and out of their house. They were like his extended family. But on the other hand maybe Burke was giving him a way out of the dilemma and was prepared not to take it any further. Maybe if they sorted it out here and now that would be the end of it. He felt that he was being cornered, but decided to give in.

"All right," he agreed, "if that's what it takes."

"I'm glad that you're being sensible about this," Fr
Burke said, smiling sourly.

"That's all right so," Tim said. Thinking that they
had finished their business, he rose to his feet.

"As far as I'm concerned," Fr Burke told him, "but
you are to see the bishop tomorrow morning at 11am."

Tim stared at Fr Burke in disbelief. He had thought
that the PP was giving him a chance to sort the problem out between them, but all the time he was only
leading him up the garden path. What a two-faced old
devil he was! Tim's temper began to simmer and his
self-control slip.

"You mean to tell me that you put me through all this
and that you had already contacted the bishop?" Tim
demanded, and before Fr Burke could say anything, he
grasped the back of the bentwood chair and thumped
it off the floor. "You're some hypocrite!" he blazed. "You
can forget all the high-minded promises you extracted
under false pretences. That malicious rumour that's
going around probably came from you or Conway, and
one of you isn't much better than the other."

Before Fr Burke had time to recover, Tim shot out
the door, nearly falling over Lizzy who was busy pol-
ishing the brass knob.

"Give your man inside a rub," he told her and
banged the heavy front door after him.

He could feel the temper thumping in his head. Fr
Burke must really have enjoyed extracting those promises out of him. *You're some fool, Brady,* he told himself.

As he passed the church door, he turned in on impulse and went up and sat into the front pew.

"Listen, hear you," he said, addressing the unseen presence on the altar, "if you think that I'm going to put up with much more of this, you're going to be minus one labourer in your vineyard. If your bishop is anything like your parish priest, it's definitely going to be curtains between us."

Tim sat for a while until he calmed down, and then he thought of his father and wondered what he would think of the situation. He decided to drive over and have a chat with him. As it was a long drive to his home town, he put a note on the door to call Fr Burke for any sick call. He drove out of the village, glad to be going home, away from the confusion that had become part of his life here.

When he pushed open the pub door, his brother, who was serving a customer, winked in welcome. He made a bee-line for the kitchen behind the pub. The last thing he felt like was a chat with old neighbours who would be all questions about how he was getting on. He knew that his father, who was busy at the other end of the pub, would follow him in. The kitchen was empty and for that he was grateful.

His father came in quietly and closed the door firmly behind him. A tall, thin man with a thatch of white hair, Dan Brady had three interests in life: his family, his customers and the GAA. Of his five sons he worried most about Tim. He was the one who had been most affected by his mother's death, and Dan had never been quite sure if he were cut out for the priesthood. Tim would either be a star turn or a disaster; there would be no middle course. Looking at his face now, it seemed as if disaster were threatening.

"What's the trouble?" his father asked, putting on the kettle and taking a chair across the table from Tim.

"That sounds as if I'm always coming home with my problems," Tim said.

"Where else would you go?" his father asked.

"I'm thinking of leaving," Tim said, and until he had put it into words he had not fully realised the possibility.

"Fill me in," his father said.

So Tim told him the whole story and his father listened without interruption. Tim was glad to get an opportunity to get it all out. It was as if in the telling he got to see things more clearly himself.

When he finished his father said, "A lot will depend on the bishop's reaction, won't it?"

"You're right," Tim agreed, "and if his reaction is anything like Burke's, I'm getting out."

CHAPTER ELEVEN

A S HE DROVE up the avenue to the bishop's palace, Tim wondered what lay ahead. Coming back down, would the decision be to remain a priest or to step back into the secular world? If he decided to get out, it would be a huge upheaval, but at the moment he had had as much as he could take of the Church and her archaic customs. In many ways he would be sorry to leave because there was much about the priesthood that he loved, but Fr Burke's charade yesterday had been the last straw. Nobody enjoyed eating humble pie, but to find out after eating it that it had served no great purpose was galling. Fr Burke was driving him crazy. Maybe if he were a proper priest, Burke would not irritate him so much. Questions without answers floated around his head as he parked at the foot of the sweeping steps.

He was pleasantly surprised when the door was opened by an old classmate who seemed delighted to see him. "I knew you were the bishop's secretary, but I didn't expect you to answer the door."

"I saw your name on the list of appointments and thought that you might like to be met by a familiar face." His friend smiled and drew him into the wide, polished hallway.

"I blotted my copybook," Tim told him. It was good to see Bernard's welcoming face instead of some grim-faced cleric.

"Heard you were practising your boxing skills."

"Good news travels fast."

"Burke was on the phone and I could hear him yelling even though I was across the table, and I followed the conversation from the bishop's comments. Of course, I was all ears when I heard Burke, because I figured out straightaway that you were in trouble."

"Is it big trouble?" Tim enquired.

"I doubt it, and the bishop is a good old skin, so you'll get a fair crack of the whip."

"That's good to hear, because I'm half thinking of leaving."

"Oh, you're overreacting," Bernard soothed, and then added thoughtfully, "but maybe if I had Burke I might be thinking the same way."

"Not in a thousand years," Tim told him. "You were born for the job."

In the seminary Bernard had been a diligent student

who never broke the rules and who was good-hearted and jolly, one of the people whom Tim had most admired. Tim was sure he would be a wonderful priest and often envied him his conviction that he was on the right path.

"You're on the dot," Bernard said, looking at his watch. "He's in there waiting for you." He pointed to a tall oak door, one of many that lined both sides of the magnificent hall. "I'll just knock and tell him you're here. My advice is to take it easy now and let the whole thing work itself out. Don't jump the gun. Everything will be fine."

Tim felt reassured by Bernard's matter-of-fact approach, but when he opened the door and beckoned him in, Tim felt a bit like the little boy whose mother scolded him when he had a row with one of his brothers.

The bishop was sitting in a wing-backed chair beside a tall window that looked out over a sweeping lawn. The tall slim man, whose silver hair edged a face where every feature was in perfect proportion, rose gracefully out of the chair and came across the room.

"You're welcome, Fr Brady," he said. "Take a seat." He pointed to a companion chair at the other side of the window. He rang a little silver bell on an adjoining mahogany table and seated himself across from Tim. The door opened and Bernard came in.

"I think that it's time for our morning break, Fr Bernard," the bishop said pleasantly, "so will you

arrange to have a tray brought to Fr Brady and myself."
Turning to Tim he asked, "Have you ever been here
before?"

"No, your Lordship," Tim told him.

"It's really a magnificent residence. It was the family
home of the Cole family for generations, one of the
lucky houses that escaped being burned in the
Troubles. After that the diocese bought it, and I'm
lucky enough to be the one to enjoy it now."

Tim felt that this aesthetic-looking man probably
appreciated in full the fine architecture of this grand
old house. It surprised him somewhat that the conversation was about the residence rather than himself, but
he was more surprised when the bishop went on to say,
"I believe that you have done a lot to brighten up your
own house in Kilmeen."

"You know the house?" Tim asked.

"Oh indeed, very well. A great friend of mine was a
curate there many years ago, so I often visited. I liked
that house."

"So do I," Tim said enthuastically. "Even though it's
small, there is a certain style about it, with the lovely
little Gothic windows and the flagged floors."

"Unfortunately the diocese has very few houses of
that calibre. Despite their faults, the landed gentry
knew how to build well and they planted fine trees." He
pointed out the window to the huge oaks that graced
the sweeping lawns. Tim thought of his republican
father and wondered if he would have considered fine

houses and trees a compensation for what had gone before.

"Your father would not concur," the bishop said mildly.

"I don't think so," Tim agreed, feeling that he had better be careful of his thoughts as this fellow could nearly see into his head.

"We all come from different backgrounds," the bishop said. "Fr Burke, now, is the only son of two teachers. They were good people who both taught in a small national school where they ruled with a rod of iron. A very religious couple, maybe a bit puritanical, and their one ambition was to have a son a priest. They thought that was what God wanted from them and they probably convinced their son of that as well. Sometimes a vocation can be a cross cast upon you by others, and the people who carry those crosses may be the martyrs of our Church."

Wait a minute now, Tim thought, *where is this conversation going? I came in here thinking that I was the wrong man in the wrong job, and here I'm being made feel sympathetic towards Burke.* He was about to say something, but remembered Bernard's advice.

"You were skilled in the boxing ring," the bishop remarked.

Now we're getting places, Tim thought.

"One of my brothers was involved in a big way and I used to tag along, and then discovered that I had a natural aptitude for it," Tim told him.

"Light on your feet, of course," the bishop commented, and then in a throwaway remark, "probably good on the dance floor as well."

Now, Tim thought, *we are definitely getting down to it!*

"I love music and dancing," he said, deciding to give it to him straight, "and I did not drop any of them when I was in the seminary. I always went dancing during the holidays."

"A commendable pursuit," the bishop said, "and did you wear your clerical garb?"

"Sometimes, but that made no difference, because it was in my own home town where everyone knew me, so I was statute barred, so to speak."

The bishop looked out over the lawn and remarked to himself more than to Tim, "That could sometimes work against you."

Tim was not quite sure where the present conversation was heading or what it had to do with the problem in hand, so he waited silently for the bishop to make the next move. When the move came it took him by surprise.

"Were you ever in love, Fr Brady?" the bishop asked. When Tim looked at him in amazement, he continued, "You know, when they put a collar around your neck, they did not put a blindfold around your eyes and a stone wall around your heart."

What is he at now? Tim wondered. *Is he laying a trap or are we having an affable discussion?* Tim decided to put all his cards on the table. "If you asked me that question a week ago, I'd have said no, but now I'm not so sure."

"What changed your mind?"

"Fr Burke," Tim said.

"Ironic," the bishop smiled.

"He has probably told you all about Kate and David Twomey."

"More about Kate than David," said the bishop, still smiling.

"I can imagine. Well, they are my best friends and that was all there was to it until Fr Burke caused me to question my motives."

"'Nothing is either bad or good but thinking makes it so.' Shakespere had it all covered, but then I suppose we could go back even further to Eve's nakedness in the garden of Eden," the bishop mused to himself.

"You see, I never had a sister," Tim told him, "so I'm not very sharp where women are concerned. Maybe what I feel for Kate is more than brotherly affection."

"Wouldn't think so," the bishop told him to his surprise. "You don't look like a man in love to me. But even if you were, it would not be the end of your clerical road. A priest who falls in love and remains faithful to his vows comes out of the experience enriched and more tolerant. And you are very lucky because the woman in question is happily married and has no interest in you other than as a friend. So you have only your own problem to deal with. For a priest to fall in love with someone who returns his feelings and is in close proximity puts a ferocious strain on the people concerned."

Why do I feel, Tim thought, *that he is speaking from experience?* He was at a loss to know what to say, so he kept his mouth firmly shut as the bishop talked on. Tim got the impression that he was talking his own thoughts out loud rather than lecturing him as he had expected.

"Being a young curate is very difficult because you can only learn by trial and error, and your errors are always very public. This frightens young priests, so they close down their emotional departments and become sanctified robots. They are afraid to be themselves, so they start to be what they think they should be and lose their fire and enthusiasm. There is no substitute for enthusiasm, and if you don't have it when you're young, you're not going to develop it in old age. Enthusiasm and love is the lifeblood of the Church."

Tim listened attentively, wondering where all this was leading. He was not sure if he was winning or losing but he thought that maybe things were not going too badly. The bishop brought him out of his assessment by asking, "What were your thoughts coming in here?"

"I was thinking of packing it in," Tim told him bluntly.

"Why exactly?" the bishop asked.

"Well, to be honest, working with Fr Burke is like being fettered," he said.

"In years to come you may look back and thank him," the bishop said.

"What?" Tim exclaimed.

"I started off with a wonderful parish priest, and afterwards when I was older and less pliable I hit a few rocks. It would have been better for me had it been the other way around. You will learn a lot from him. Look well at him. He will teach you how you think a curate should not be treated. And yet there are people in Kilmeen who have great respect for him. It always amazes me, Fr Tim, how tolerant the people are and how intolerant we the clergy are. There are far more disagreements between the clergy than there are between the people and the clergy."

"Is that right?" Tim asked in surprise.

"Yes, I have more disagreeing clergy in here to me than complaining laity, and that tells a lot about us," the bishop said. "If we were less concerned with ourselves and more so with our parishioners, it would be better for all of us."

"In other words, you're telling me to overcome my attitude to Fr Burke and concentrate on our parishioners."

"Your parishioners are your priority. Maybe your choice of sermon in view of that old parish feud was not the wisest, but then I'm not saying that it should not have been given. It is only when you are on the ground in a parish that you can best judge these things."

145

"Maybe I should have held my horses," Tim agreed.

"The other side of the coin then," the bishop continued, "is that you were dealing with a real live issue in the parish. It is very relevant to people's lives. There is always a danger that the people could regard the Church as irrelevant to ordinary living. So in that sense you were right."

"Hard to win, isn't it?" Tim said.

"One can only do one's best, and you are doing a lot of good for the young of the parish. But it might be a good idea to spread out your visiting time over more houses. People like the priest to call, and if you have built up a relationship, they will come to you when they're in trouble. That's our greatest calling, to be there for people when they need us. But I'm not advising you to neglect your friends. We priests need our friends; they take the loneliness out of our station."

He is giving me the whole message in small doses, Tim thought, *without even ruffling my feathers.* But the messages were being delivered nevertheless. Tim knew that he was a low profile bishop, but he had the name of looking after his priests well. The possibility of leaving had melted from his mind and he knew that there was going to be no censure from the bishop. To say that he was astonished by the ways things had gone was putting it mildly. The bishop was a surprise packet.

Just then Bernard came in bearing a tray. When he set it on a table, the bishop looked at it and said, "Fetch another cup for yourself, Fr Bernard, and we'll have our little respite together. After all, you and Fr Tim are old friends."

Fr Bernard, who had his back to the bishop, gave Tim a conspiratol wink of triumph and disappeared back out the door.

"A great lad," the bishop said, "dedicated, devoted and with a big lump of common sense to keep him sane and, dare I say it, blessed with that little bit of dullness that makes life bearable."

Tim looked at him questioningly and he smiled.

"That surprises you to hear me say that, doesn't it? You may even think that it's a wee bit disloyal, but the likes of Fr Bernard will keep the Church going: the dedicated and the understated who will always be there to keep the show on the road. On any farm it is the plough horses who are the viable units, not the hunters, who may have patches of brilliance but are also quite capable of turning tail and scaling out over the ditch with a scatter of sods behind them."

Tim felt that he might be in the hunter class and that it was no compliment. He was glad when Bernard returned and the conversation broadened out into talk of their days in the seminary and the whereabouts of all the other students now.

After a while the bishop rose and excused himself but told them, "Take your time and make the most of this opportunity. You should make arrangements to meet again. It's a pity to loose touch with old friends."

When they were alone together, Tim stretched his

legs, breathed a sigh of relief and said to Bernard, "Thank God that's over."

"I told you that you'd be fine," Bernard smiled. "I've learned a lot about him since I came here, and if we had more like him we'd be flying."

"I think that he wants us to keep in touch so that you can keep an eye on me."

"A good idea," Bernard laughed.

"That was a rather unusual session, very different from Burke yesterday," Tim declared.

"The different faces of the Church," Fr Bernard agreed.

"I'm beginning to realise that it has many," Tim told him, "and it looks as if I'm going to be one of them for another while anyway."

CHAPTER TWELVE

A S SHE LAID the table for the dinner, Martha thought back over her conversation with Mark and Agnes a few day previously. It annoyed her that they were thinking of signing over the farm to Peter. It exasperated her to be passed over as if she were of no consequence. After all, she was the daughter of the house and surely had some rights. She resented the attitude that men carried more weight where land inheritance was concerned. She should have the same rights as Mark.

Nellie Phelan had thought of her own daughter when making her will and had given her rights in Mossgrove. It irked her that Nellie Phelan had provided better for her daughter's future than her own mother was going to do for her. When she thought about it, Nellie Phelan's will was very far-seeing. It had prevented herself from selling Mossgrove, and she was glad of that now. She wondered what else was in that will. Ned had never got around to making one, so could there be any other clause in Nellie's will that she should know about? Maybe the time had come to visit Mr Hobbs and find out the lie of the land. If she had gone to him after Ned's death she would have spared herself a lot of trouble. How well Kate had been clever enough to check it out.

She had not gone in the intervening years because she was reluctant to confront Hobbs, who by all accounts was a wily old bird and also who would not have forgotten that she had gone to his opposite number. But after the conversation with Mark and Agnes, she had decided to pay him a visit. She had gone into the village and rung him, and she had an appointment for this afternoon. The secretary had tried to put her on the long finger, but she had insisted that it was urgent.

She intended telling nobody, but would let them think that she was just going into the village. Instead she would take the bus over to Ross and be back in time for the cows. It was annoying her as well that Peter had made no reference to the fact that Agnes and Mark had offered them the meadows. They would have to be cut soon, so did he intend to just go ahead without even telling her? He was really taking things into his own hands. She was going to bring it up now during the dinner. Davy was home until after his grandmother's funeral, so there would only be Jack and themselves. Whatever Peter was up to, Jack was in on it.

They came in the back door with a clatter of conversation. *Do they ever shut up,* Martha wondered, *and what on earth do they find to talk about all day every day?*

As they seated themselves at the table, Peter asked, "Are you going to the funeral?"

"Weren't you all there yesterday evening?" she said.

"Well, it would be nice if you went today," Peter told her.

"We'll see."

"There was a mighty crowd last night," Jack remarked.

"Waste of time," Martha told him.

"What do you mean by that?" Peter demanded.

"When you're dead, you're dead," Martha replied, "and gawking neighbours won't do you much good."

"But what about the family?" Peter wanted to know.

"Better off without half the busybodies," she told him.

"I don't agree with you," Peter retorted.

"Nothing new," she said curtly.

"I remember the people who were here when Dad died," Peter said thoughtfully, "and even though I thought at the time they were no help, I think now that they were."

"Conditioning."

"Well, your approach to funerals was not much good

at the time," Peter declared, "burying your head and nearly selling us out."

"All water under the bridge," Jack intervened. "Those days are long gone."

"But you never forget days like those," Peter asserted. "They are still clear in my mind."

"Better get on with today," Martha told him briskly, "not be wasting time looking over your shoulder at the past. We can't live there."

"How can you talk like that when you're living in a house like this, that's so full of our past?"

"Maybe that's why I think it," she told him. "This place is like living in a Phelan museum."

"That's why I love this house," he said. "I feel that Dad is still part of it."

As she listened Martha visualised the reaction when she would tell him that they were moving out. There was going to be an explosion of opposition, but she would be ready for it. Now there was a more immediate problem.

"Why did you not tell me that Mark and Nana Agnes said that we could have their meadows?" she demanded.

"But surely you knew that they'd give them to us?" he asked in surprise.

"You don't know anything until you're told," she said sharply.

"Well, I assumed that you would discuss it with them as well."

"Well, I didn't get the chance, and when I did it was to be told that it was all arranged," she said.

"There was no arranging in it; they offered and I accepted, and I'm getting a loan of Nolans' tractor to do the cutting."

"You asked the Nolans for a loan of their tractor without even discussing it with me?" she demanded angrily.

"There was no asking," he told her. "Tom Nolan offered, so what should I have done — refused him to keep you happy?"

She was glad when the dinner was over and she had the kitchen to herself. When everything was tidied up to her satisfaction, she went upstairs to get ready. She intended to dress well, as that always made her feel more self-assured, but at the same time she did not want to draw any attention to herself. Jack and Peter would assume that she was going to the funeral and that suited her fine. They could find out afterwards that she had not been there, and by then it would not matter. She did not go into the village to catch the bus but waited for it at the end of the road.

When she saw Mr Hobbs she could understand why he was known as Old Mr Hobbs, even though there was no young Mr Hobbs. Everything about him was aged and fragile, and he wore a slightly bewildered air which she knew was entirely misleading. He was extremely tall, thin and courteous, with faded blond hair trailing along the sides of a completely bald head. His clothes

Alice Taylor

seemed to have been tailored for someone two sizes smaller, and tiny gold spectacles perched precariously at the end of a long thin nose.

"Well, Mrs Phelan," he enquired, putting his long thin fingers together in a praying position and peering out over his spectacles, "what can we do for you?"

His pale blue eyes coolly appraised her across a large oak desk, and Martha felt that he intended to do as little as possible. On the desk lay one green file that she assumed held the Phelan documents. The sight of the file had a strange effect on her. In there was the will of Nellie Phelan, with whom she had shared a house but whom she had never liked. She did not understand why, but even before she had moved into Mossgrove she had resented Ned's mother, and now the feeling was coming back. Nellie Phelan might be dead, but she was still alive in a file that enshrined her wishes. This old man, who looked like a fossil but whose legal brain was clever and calculating, had kept her wishes entombed in his oak desk. All these thoughts flitted through her mind, but she was not going to let this austere geriatric unnerve her.

She sat well back into her chair, straightened her back and looked directly at him.

"I would like to know what's in Nellie Phelan's will," she demanded.

"Very wise," he said evenly, making no attempt to open the file.

There was complete silence in the room. While

154

waiting for Mr Hobbs to begin, she looked around and concluded that every item in the room looked as if it had lain undisturbed for years. Mr Hobbs seemed quite content to sit still, his long bony fingers now playing soundless notes on his desk.

"Well?" Martha demanded.

"Well indeed," he refrained.

"How long does it take to open that file?" she demanded.

"It has not been opened for eight years," he said mildly.

"And then at the request of my sister-in-law, Kate."

"No," he said quietly

"How do you mean, no?" she snapped.

"Your sister-in-law did not request to see her mother's will," he told her.

"But how else did she find out about the right-of-residency clause that prevented me from selling Mossgrove?" she asked.

"Because I told her," he said.

"So you sent for her instead of me, which to my way of thinking would have been a more correct procedure," she said.

He sat still, looking at her, and though he never twitched a muscle she could sense that he was annoyed. He sniffed lightly and rubbed his chin as if pondering the peculiarities of life, and then said in the same tone of voice, "You had sought other counsel and it would have been unethical of me to have interfered. However, in order to avoid your public embarrassment, I told Kate Phelan about the clause in the will when she came here with Mr Twomey about the school. She did not ask about the will, but because the Phelans have been valued clients for many years, I intervened before the farm was sold. If it had been sold, there would have been the public embarrassment of the clause overturning the sale. By strictly legal terms, that should have been the course of action. Miss Phelan, however, was very anxious that you should not be upset, so I informed your legal representative."

Martha swallowed hard. So Kate had just come across the knowledge by chance.

"Kate Phelan has not seen her mother's will?" she asked.

"That's correct," he told her.

"Has anybody?" she asked.

"No."

"Why?" she demanded.

"Nobody asked," he told her.

"Don't you think that's extraordinary?" she exclaimed.

"Not in the least," he told her.

"Why do you alone have the right to know what's in there?" she demanded, pointing to the file.

"I have no rights whatsoever," he said quietly. "Only the people who made the will have rights, and my job is to protect them."

"And what about the people who come after them?" she demanded.

"My job is also to serve them, and a good will does that. It also protects the rights of the unborn, as it did in this case."

"Well, I think that the only important people in a will are the living," she asserted.

"The living can very quickly become the dead, Mrs Phelan."

In the present circumstances, she considered it an ill-chosen statement.

"Ned never made a will," she said.

"Not unusual in a young, able-bodied man," he told her, "so his mother's will still stands."

"Has it got implications for Mossgrove today?" she asked.

"Certainly."

"Dictating from the grave," she said scornfully.

"In anything she decided she was advised by me," he told her.

"Do you like playing God?" she asked.

"Sometimes we get it right, between us." He smiled cryptically. "He is the silent partner."

"Do you have to go into consultation with Him as to when I get to see this will?" she asked, pointing to the green file on the table.

"No, I can make that decision on my own," he assured her.

"Well," she demanded, "what are we waiting for?"

"Your children," he said
"What!"
"Yes," he told her evenly, "it would be desirable to have them present."
"Why?" she demanded.
"Because it affects them too," he told her. "Actually it was opportune that you came in today, because I would have been writing to you."
Martha was alarmed. What on earth was this old bird up to? Nothing good, she was sure.
"So we must come back together," she said.
"Correct. You can make an appointment with my secretary on the way out."
Later, as she walked slowly up the road to Mossgrove, she churned the whole interview over in her mind. So Kate had not gone to Old Hobbs to poke out things about Nellie's will. She had come across it by pure chance, and when she had discovered the stipulation in the will, she had not taken advantage of the situation and told the family. If Peter had known it would have been the last straw between them. She had misjudged Kate in that.
But what the hell has Old Hobbs up his sleeve now? Martha wondered. There was no doubt but he was hell-bent on looking after the wishes of the dead Phelans and making sure that Mossgrove was safe. The prospect of Peter accompanying her on the next visit disturbed her. She felt now that it was inevitable that he would find out about the right-of-residency clause

and that she could not sell Mossgrove. It had passed through her mind to ask Old Hobbs not to mention it, but as he was not sympathetic towards her, he would probably have refused. It would be the final wedge between herself and Peter.

CHAPTER THIRTEEN

THERE WAS SILENCE in the kitchen but for the ticking of the clock and the occasional rustle of the newspaper as Peter straightened it to read further down a column. He was stretched out on the sofa beneath the back window through which the evening sunlight slanted. His hair kept falling across his eyes, and every so often he tossed his head like a pony keeping flies at bay. As Martha caught the movement out of the corner of her eye, a memory of Ned darted through her.

With a frown of intense concentration on her face, Nora sat writing at the table in the dying light of the kitchen. Martha darned a sock in the well of the front window, working the needle back and forth through the cross threads, slowly weaving away the hole. When it was indistinguishable from the rest of the heel, the sharp snip of the scissors cracked into the silence of the kitchen. She eased the sock off her hand and examined it for further signs of wear and tear. The toe area was about to come asunder.

"Peter, you have toes like meat cleavers," she told him.

"My mother's anatomy." He grinned good humouredly as he lowered the paper and sheets of it floated on to the floor. Before she had time to tell him pick them up, he retrieved them saying, "Right, right, you don't like untidy newspapers. You like to get the paper in the order in which it should be read."

"Nothing wrong with that," she told him, holding up the darning needle between herself and the window to see the eye more clearly to ease the dark brown wool through it.

"Is your vision fading, Mother?" he asked.

"I'll do that for you, Mom, if you like," Nora offered, pushing back her chair, but Martha said, "One minute. I think I have it, Nora. That's it, it's through."

"It's always good to stretch oneself," Peter proclaimed.

"Could you stretch yourself, so, and put on the kettle for the supper?" Martha asked him.

"Women's work," he announced, watching Nora out of the corner of his eye. He did not have long to wait for a reaction.

She jumped up and crash-landed on top of him, intent on pulling his hair, but he caught her hands and they rolled around the sagging sofa while she told him, "You're off the ark, set in prehistoric times."

"He said that specially to annoy you," Martha told her.

"I know, but he's not going to get away with it," Nora yelled as she tussled with Peter to get him off the sofa.

As Martha watched their horseplay, she thought of Mark and herself; they never had that comradeship. Since these two were children they had looked out for each other. Nora was kind and gentle while Peter was brash and direct, but still there was an understanding between them. If push came to shove between Peter and herself, she was not sure on whose side Nora would come down. Hopefully it would never come to that. Tonight she would tell them about going over to see Mr Hobbs tomorrow. She had left telling them as late as possible because she knew that Peter would be full of questions, and the shorter run he had into the interview the better.

As they sat around the table, Peter was describing in great detail to Nora how much faster the tractor was at cutting the hay, but Nora was preoccupied with a point that Jack and herself were after discussing.

"But if there was a pheasant hatching in the middle of the high grass, the tractor would be going too fast for anybody to see it and it would be killed."

"Yourself and Jack have all these notions about caring for the wildlife, but, Norry, we can't put them before us, and if we did we'd never move forward at all," Peter told her.

"I still think it's not right," Nora argued.

"Well, that's the way life is."

"Well, we don't have to like it that way."

"You're all nicey-nicey but you're as stubborn as a mule," Peter informed her.

"You've got to stand up for what you believe in," Nora responded.

The argument went around in circles for a few more minutes, and when Martha judged that they were running out of steam she cut in, "If you're finished sorting out the balance of nature, I have interesting news for the two of you. Tomorrow the three us are going over to Mr Hobbs the solicitor; we have an appointment for three o'clock."

They both looked at her in amazement, and as she had expected Peter shot the first question.

"For what?" he demanded.

"I don't know," she told him.

"But how do you know that he wanted to see us?" he demanded.

"I was over about something else and he told me," she said.

"You were over about something else?" he said in a puzzled voice. "What took you over to him?"

"Well, I wanted to know about the family wills," she said.

"But Dad made no will, so there was only Nana Nellie's giving Dad the farm, and we know about that for years," he said, looking at her curiously.

"But nobody had actually seen it," she told him.

"Didn't you see it after Dad dying, surely?" he asked.

"Well, I didn't," she admitted.

"But why?" he demanded.

"Because I went to another solicitor," she told him.

"Oh." She could see him thinking back to that time, and he continued slowly, "That was because you were going to sell and you knew that Old Hobbs would advise against it."

"Maybe," she admitted.

"There's no maybe about it," he told her, "you really went off the tracks that time and nearly took us all with you."

"That was because Mom was so upset at the time," Nora intervened, "and Jack says that it was quite understandable in the circumstances."

"Well, hooray for understanding Jack," Peter said angrily, "but if Mossgrove had been sold out from under him, he might not have finished up so compassionate."

"Well, it wasn't," Nora told him, "so why are we arguing about something that never happened?"

"Because the idea of it, so soon after Dad dying, nearly killed me with him. The thought of the Conways coming in here was enough to make every Phelan in Kilmeen graveyard turn over."

"Well, it will never happen now," Nora declared.

"That's for sure, even though Matt Conway intends to rough us up a bit over the river meadows. He was stone mad after Fr Brady's sermon," Peter said, "but Brady beat the lard out of him. He took on the wrong man there."

"I wonder will Fr Brady be reprimanded?" Martha asked, glad of the respite from talk about the visit to Mr Hobbs.

"Well, he was at training last night and he was in great form, so I'd say he is all right," Peter said.

"I wouldn't like to be a priest," Nora decided.

"You're not likely to have that problem thrust upon you," Peter told her dismissively, and continued in a perplexed voice, "But what on earth could Mr Hobbs want the three of us for?"

"There must be something in Nana Nellie's will that affects the three of us," Nora concluded.

"Brilliant deduction. Did he give you any hint?" Peter asked Martha.

"None whatsoever."

"But what made you decide to go to see him now after so many years?" Peter asked, looking searchingly at his mother. "You must have had some reason. You never do anything off the top of your head like me; you think it all out carefully."

"Maybe Mom got a feeling in her bones that the time was right," Nora told him.

"She doesn't operate like that," Peter insisted.

"Maybe Nora is right," Martha said, glad to side-step the issue, but like Peter and Nora she, too, was very curious to know what was in Nellie's will. Old Hobbs was a difficult man to fathom. Nora was right about the feeling in her bones, but that had to do with her next visit to Hobbs, not the last one. She felt in her bones that the news might not be favourable to her, but she was less worried about that than the prospect of Peter finding out the details about her attempt to sell Mossgrove. For the last eight years it had been a bone of contention between them even though he thought that she had changed her mind and decided against selling. It would really turn him against her when he found out the truth tomorrow.

Just then they heard Bran barking out in the yard.

"Someone coming," Nora announced, and when Bran stopped barking, "It's someone he knows."

They heard the back door into the scullery opening, and when Kate's dark head appeared around the door into the kitchen, Nora smiled in delight.

"Aunty Kate, you're very late. We thought you were Matt Conway."

"Heaven forbid," Kate said.

"You were delivering a baby back this way?" Peter guessed.

"No, Peter, I called back to Davy's mother. She is a bit down and out since her mother died," Kate said.

"Davy was saying that," Peter told her. "He thinks that it has brought back the upset of his father's death."

"He could be right," Kate agreed. "It was a terrible tragedy the way he was killed by Nolans' bull. Biddy was left with a house full of young children, and she had to keep going then, so maybe now she is double grieving."

"Will you have a cup of tea?" Martha offered. "We're just having it."

"Thanks," Kate said. "Any move from across the river?"

"No," Peter answered. "All quiet on the western front."

"I hope that you're keeping an eye out for him," Kate cautioned. "I wouldn't underestimate him."

"Well, we can't let ourselves become obsessed with it or we wouldn't move at all," Peter told her.

"I suppose you're right," Kate agreed. "Did you hear that Rodney Jackson is here for a few weeks?"

"Is he?" Nora said eagerly. "Is he staying with you, Aunty Kate?"

"As usual," Kate told her. "After all, we owe him so much that's the least we can do."

"The least you can do!" Nora echoed. "I wouldn't mind him staying here. I think he's gorgeous!"

"I suppose he's pretty dishy, all right, but he's a bit long in the tooth for you, Nora."

"I like older men," Nora sighed, "and it's hardly fair that you have him and Uncle David all to yourself. When I was in first year, I had a big crush on Uncle David, all the girls had, but I'm over it now."

"Nora, you're a pain in the butt," Peter told her.

"Have you any news here?" Kate asked before an argument started.

"Oh, we have," Nora told her. "Tomorrow we're going over to Mr Hobbs in Ross to hear something in Nana Nellie's will."

Watching Kate's face, Martha knew that she was startled. She had always assumed that Kate knew what was in the will, but now she knew differently. Hobbs had them all in the dark. She was glad that Kate knew nothing more than herself. Now, instead of her feeling an outsider with the Phelans, they were on level footing. Could it be possible that Jack knew something? But that was unlikely, because what Jack knew, Kate knew.

"Did Old Hobbs send for you?" Kate asked. There was a slight pause, and Peter and Nora looked at Martha, who said briefly, "No, I was over about something else," and she knew by Kate's face that she was wondering how much Old Hobbs had told her about her own visit. *Why do wills always make people feel uneasy,* she wondered, *or is it only when family relationships are strained?* But then there were probably few families without some inner friction going on.

"Did Fr Brady recover from the upheaval with Matt Conway?" she asked Kate, and was amused to sense that Kate was slightly embarrassed by the question. So Kate had heard the gossip about them.

"It all sorted itself out," Kate said. "The bishop was pretty decent about the whole thing."

"He had to go to the bishop?" Peter said in surprise. "So Fr Burke pulled the plug on him."

"Apparently, but the bishop was a lot more understanding than Fr Burke," Kate said.

"I should hope so," Peter declared. "We'd be lost without him in the club. Davy thinks that he should start a boxing club."

"It could happen," Kate smiled, "but I had better be off because I'll call to Jack on the way home."

"He's having problems trying to balance the advantage of the speed of tractor cutting against the damage to the wildlife," Peter said.

"I could see Jack having a problem with that all right."

"I'm having a problem with it, too," Nora told her.

"Don't mind you," Peter told her.

"How would you like to be a pheasant with your two legs cut off?" Nora demanded.

"That doesn't happen. The pheasants aren't that bloody stupid that they'd wait for that to happen to them."

"But what about their eggs or their babies?" Nora protested.

"I think you've gone over all this before," Martha said, "but while you do it again, I'll walk up a bit with Aunty Kate and the two of you can tidy up."

Martha knew that Kate was amazed that she had offered to accompany her up the boreen. It was the first time she had walked up with Kate. Ned always had, and she had often envied their closeness as she watched them walk away together. Now that she saw the same closeness between Peter and Nora, she could better understand the bond between Ned and Kate. The offer was a gesture of friendship. She appreciated deeply that Kate had not used her mother's will to make life difficult. She was not so sure that she would have been that kind in the circumstances.

"I was very impressed that Fr Brady took on that sermon," Martha began as they walked along. "It showed great courage."

"More courage than wisdom, I think," Kate said ruefully. "It ran him into big trouble."

"Sometimes you have to do things you don't want to because they need to be done," Martha said.

"Well, maybe," Kate answered, "but everything worked out for the better. He found the bishop a bit of a revelation, to say the least of it."

"Sarah Jones probably had the bishop filled in on the background," Martha said.

"Possibly," Kate agreed.

"They go back a long ways, don't they?" Martha said, and because Kate seemed reluctant to say anything, she continued, "I visited the Miss Jacksons as well as Mark when we were young, and the bishop was a visitor there often. Sometimes Sarah Jones would be invited because she was an old friend of the bishop's."

"The Miss Jacksons knew him since he was a curate, didn't they?" Kate asked. "Strange the way all our lives intertwine."

"That's because we're all living in such a small bowl,"

Martha said. "Sometimes we get knotted together and nearly choke each other."

"I hope that everything turns out all right tomorrow," Kate said quietly.

"Tomorrow should be an interesting day."

CHAPTER FOURTEEN

J ACK SAT INSIDE his window in the dusk and looked
down over the fields. He kept the hedge in front of
his window cut low so that he could enjoy the view
when he sat at the table. Nolans' cows were gathered
in the corner beyond his hedge, some already lying
down contentedly chewing the cud while others grazed
beside them, having the last few bites before finally settling for the night. *They are like our ourselves*, Jack
thought. *Some of them can never have enough while others
are more relaxed and ready to take things easy.*

Beyond Nolans' farm he could see down over the village where the lights were beginning to come on in the
houses. He had been without electricity so long himself that now, even though he had it, he preferred to
wait until all God's light was gone before he turned it
on. It was pleasant sitting in the dusk and watching the

shadows gathering in the corners of the fields. The darkening horizon was still shot through with streaks of crimson. Earlier on there had been a wonderful sunset, a ball of orange which had disappeared below the horizon shooting back rays of brilliant red. Tomorrow would be another good day.

The trees and bushes were taking on strange shapes, and it was good to watch the sky darken and the first stars come out. The smell of his flowers, some of which came into their own at this time of day, wafted in the open window. His old favourite, the night-scented stock, was the lady of the dusk.

He picked up his pipe from the deep windowsill and massaged the palm of his hand with the bowl of the fine briar. This was a special pipe. On the day of Ned's accident Nora, who was about ten at the time, had money in her pocket to buy her father a pipe. Long afterwards the money was found knotted up in her small white handkerchief in the pocket of her torn coat. She had kept the money for a long time under her pillow, her last link with her father, and then one day she had gone to the village and bought this pipe for Jack. It was his greatest treasure, a physical connnection between Ned, Nora and himself.

There was great satisfaction in cutting the little shreds of tobacco off the square plug. He rubbed them gently against his palm and sniffed the aromatic whiff. He eased the tobacco into the bowl and then cracked a match that threw his pipe into a little pool of light.

Once the match touched the tobacco, he drew deeply and the bowl of his pipe glowed red. Putting the cover back on, he settled deep into his chair to savour his smoke.

Smoking his pipe and thinking things out always went together in his mind. Now he cast his mind back over the day. He had suspected that Martha had something on her mind all day and now he wondered what it was. Actually, she had not been herself since the day of Davy's grandmother's funeral. Peter and himself had thought that she had gone to the funeral, and she had left them assume that, but from something that Davy had remarked, he realised that they were mistaken. So where had she been? Wherever it was, it hadn't done her much good. Something had her upset, and it was not that easy to upset Martha.

He found his mind rambling back over the years and became so immersed in his thoughts that he was not sure if a figure had flitted past the window or if he had imagined it, but when he heard the latch being raised he tensed in his chair. When Kate's head came around the door, he breathed a sigh of relief.

"God, Kate, I thought for one minute that you were Conway," he breathed.

"That's twice in the one night." she exclaimed. "Nora thought the same thing when I went in below."

"He must be taking our peace of mind," Jack sighed.

"What are you doing sitting here in the dark?" Kate asked. "I nearly decided that you were gone to bed when there was no light, but then I thought, 'I bet he is sitting in there looking out the window.'"

"I love the sunset," Jack told her. "Magnificent this evening. Watching it is as good as praying."

"Jack, the most amazing thing happened below this evening," Kate told him. "Martha actually walked up the boreen with me."

"Oh boy!" Jack exclaimed. "That's one for the book."

"I had to come in to tell you. If I told David, he would wonder what I was on about."

"That was the first crack in the ice after twenty-two years," Jack declared.

"Wasn't it just that?" Kate confirmed.

"What could have brought it on?" Jack wondered. "She hasn't been herself with a few days, since the day of Davy's grandmother's funeral. She let us think that she was there, but from something Davy said I know that she wasn't."

"Do you know where she was, Jack? She was over with Old Hobbs."

"What was she doing over with him?" Jack exclaimed, and then he thought back over the conversation between Peter and Martha about the Lehane meadows.

"Is she wondering about the home farm?" Jack said slowly. "I knew when it came to an argument between Peter and herself about the meadows that there was something else bothering her. Would Mark and Agnes be deciding to give that land to Peter? Martha would resent that. Of course she knows now for sure that you knew all along about the clause in the will. She would appreciate that you never mentioned it, which is more than can be said for me."

"Did you say it to her, Jack?"

"Well, it slipped out one day after a rough session between Peter and herself. You know, Kate, I have one dread, that some day she will push him so far and he will be gone. You know what Peter is like. He brought the Phelan quick temper, and he could fly off the handle one day and be out the gate. Wouldn't we be in a right mess then, with me in my seventies. I know Martha is only skirting forty, but there are none of us getting younger and we need young blood around the place, otherwise we'll be like an old people's home in a few years' time."

"Pity Martha wouldn't hear you," Kate told him.

"Oh, I know that she is full of life now, but you need the young coming up on the land. We did not rear Peter for the gate; we reared him for Mossgrove."

"I can't see Peter walking out on it," Kate said.

"There are some fair blow-ups below there sometimes, and the half of them are all about nothing. If only she would give him his head a bit. Sure, Ned was running the whole show at his age."

"Different woman of the house back then," Kate sighed.

"That's for sure."

"I nearly forgot to tell you the next exciting bit of news: the three of them, Martha, Peter and Nora, are to go over to Mr Hobbs tomorrow."

"What's that about?" Jack wondered.

"Something about Nellie's will, and the three of them must be there for it," Kate said.

"Boys, that's a bit of a surprise," Jack declared. "Nellie must have put in some other proviso."

"You mean Old Hobbs put it in," Kate told him.

"Well, yes, but they would only have put it in for the good of the Phelans and Mossgrove," Jack decided.

"Hope that it will not put Martha's nose out of joint, now when she is just starting to thaw out," Kate said thoughtfully

"That will was made when Ned was getting married and Mossgrove was supposed to be signed over to him, but Hobbs had some other way of doing things. So far he has been proved right, and I think that Martha would agree now. That could be the reason for the thaw. Peter didn't know about tomorrow when I was leaving, I'd say," Jack surmised. "It wouldn't be like him not to tell me."

"Sure, of course, he'd tell you. Peter thinks that you're the next thing to God," Kate told him.

"It would be like Martha to give him a short running at it," Jack decided.

"Maybe better that way," Kate said.

"Well, I hope to God that whatever is in that will that Peter will be more settled after it."

"It was made before he was born," Kate said slowly. "Strange when you think about that, isn't it?"

"But little changes could have been added over the years."

"The law is a strange thing," Kate mused.

They sat inside the window looking out into the moonlit fields where the cows were now dark shadows in the corner. Occasionally one of them coughed or made a snuffling noise that accentuated the quietness. Jack liked the way Kate could sit with you in silence. Herself and Nora had that in common, a trait that they had inherited from Nellie Phelan. She had been a very comforting presence, calm and wise, and Jack felt that whatever was in her will would be good for them all in the long run. Ned and the family had been well served by her, and only he and Kate, and probably Sarah Jones, knew what she had had to put up with from Martha. It was good to see now that Kate had no bitterness towards Martha, despite often having been made to feel a stranger in her old home. He knew that Kate had sometimes been deeply hurt and yet she had put it all behind her. She was obviously very happy with David. Jack was praying constantly that a child would make an appearance, even though he felt that the tide was running out. Surely Nellie, wherever she was, would not let him down. Kate deserved that, after all she had done for the parish with the new school, and he knew that she went above and beyond her call of duty as district nurse. She was back and forth to Ellen Shine every day since her

179

mother had died. Poor Ellen seemed to have gone under a dark cloud and was finding it hard to shift it.

"How's Ellen Shine?" he asked now.

"Not great. You know, the strange thing is that her mother was old and her death was expected, but still Ellen is taking it very badly."

"She never gave herself time to mourn Den when he died. She kept going, almost pretending that it never happened, so maybe this time she is double mourning," Jack suggested.

"So it was from you that Davy got that understanding," Kate said, "because I was surprised when he came up with it. It's helping him to help Ellen."

"Sometimes an old head is useful around the place," Jack declared.

"That's what Sarah Jones told Fr Brady when she was advising him about cutting down his house calls to us," Kate told him.

"So you heard the gossip," Jack said in an annoyed voice.

"Even the PP had it," Kate said.

"Oh, for God's sake, he had every stir from Lizzy."

"You knew that she had it?" Kate asked.

"I did, Sarah told me," Jack admitted.

"So Sarah decided to take things in hand?" Kate asked.

"She did. How did Fr Brady take it?" Jack asked.

"Fine, and strangely enough the bishop had the same idea," Kate mused.

"Do you think that he was advised?" Jack smiled in the darkness.

"Well, if he was she did a mighty job, because Fr Tim was delighted with him," Kate said.

"The bishop was always sound as a bell. I remember him years ago when Sarah was housekeeping for him."

"Isn't friendship a wonderful relationship?"

"In many ways more lasting than love."

He sensed Kate hesitate for a moment and then she said, "You loved Nellie, didn't you?"

In all the years that Kate and himself had known each other, it had never been mentioned, but here in the soft darkness of the summer night it was the sharing of a loving that they had both known about.

"She brought joy into my life," he told her. "Doing things with Nellie took the drudgery out of work. Even in school she was special. I was working here before she married your father, and when the drinking took him over I was glad to be there for her and to keep Mossgrove going."

"I always knew that there was something special between you," Kate told him. "When I was growing up it made life warmer at home. Funny, you know, Ned was totally unaware of it, and it was the day before he was killed that we discussed it for the first time. I think that he was glad to know it."

Jack felt the tears come into his eyes to remember the two people whom he had loved so dearly. Part of him had died with Nellie, and he had thought that he could never again feel such pain until Ned had his accident. To bury the generation younger than you was unnatural. It shook your foundations. But it was good to have Peter and Nora in Mossgrove now. As much as Peter was a mixture of his mother and his grandfather, Billy Phelan, Jack was beginning to think recently that in the heel of the hunt he was going to be a second Edward Phelan. Strange how the back-breeding broke out, skipping two generations and here again now in the third.

"You have been interwoven through so many Phelan lives," Kate's voice came gently.

"They have all been good to me," Jack said.

"You are more Mossgrove than any of us," Kate told him.

"We're only all caretakers, passing through," Jack said with a sigh. "We can only hope that the next generation will pass on what we give them."

"You have a great belief in the continuity of things. I think that you passed that on to me. Rodney Jackson, even though he was born in America, has it as well about Kilmeen."

"He is one of the best things that ever happened to Kilmeen," Jack declared. "Even myself, who is a total ignoramus where painting is concerned, can appreciate all those paintings on the walls of the school. As a matter of fact, earlier on as I watched that sunset, I envied Mark his talent."

"Jack, we'll have you with a brush and canvas when

you retire," Kate teased him as she pushed back her chair.

"I'll die in harness," Jack told her as he followed her out the door and along the narrow path to the little gate. Her small black Morris Minor was parked outside.

"Do you think that I should offer to drive them to Ross tomorrow?" she asked Jack. "I thought of it but was afraid that Martha would think that I was pushing myself on her."

"I'd offer anyway," he told her. "She can always say no."

"Grand; I'll run back early in the morning and put it as diplomatically as I can," she smiled.

When Kate had gone, Jack remained leaning on the gate thinking. It had come as a bit of a surprise when Kate had mentioned his feeling for Nellie, but he was glad to know that she understood. He had always hoped that Nellie had loved him, and Kate seemed to have no doubt about it. It was a good feeling. Nellie was gone, but while he walked the fields of Mossgrove she was still with him.

This time tomorrow night they would know if the provision in her will would change life in Mossgrove.

CHAPTER FIFTEEN

WHEN MARTHA AWOKE she lay in bed considering the day ahead because this morning she felt the need to do a bit of thinking. The bad patch after Ned's death had lodged deep within her a fear of lying there. During those terrible days she had been unable to get herself out of bed and her inner demons had almost destroyed her. That was all in the past, but she was conscious that those demons could be awakened again, and they were nearer the surface early in the morning. This morning, however, she was not giving way to morbid thinking but wondering what the day ahead would bring.

The thing that she did not want to happen was for the gap between herself and Peter to become wider. What was it with herself and Peter? They simply scrope

off each other. It had always been like that since he was
a little boy. When Ned was alive, he was able to pour oil
on their troubled waters, but after his death their relationship had deteriorated. Maybe she had been too
distraught to be able to help Peter when he most
needed her, but then she had not known what she was
doing herself. Their relationship would probably have
recovered in time but for her attempt to sell
Mossgrove. Peter was devastated by that. Only the fact
that she had changed her mind gave her some saving
grace in his eyes. Today he would learn that she had
not changed her mind but that his grandmother's will
had changed her mind for her.

She had always found Peter difficult, but once he
became a teenager he was absolutely impossible. If he
got too much headway, she felt that he would walk all
over her. She knew that Jack thought that she was
wrong, but then Jack and Peter could always discuss
their differences and come to an agreement. If only it
could be like that between herself and Peter. Her wedding photograph was on the wall at the end of the bed,
and at first glance it could be Peter in the picture. He
looked so like Ned, but inside he was not in the least
bit like him.

She looked around the room, the only one in
Mossgrove that she ever felt to be completely hers. The
big old timber bed had been Edward Phelan's, but
strangely enough that did not put her off it. He was the
one Phelan whom she might have understood. Jack

always said he was tough and straight, and she liked
people like that. Maybe if Nellie Phelan had had some
of his toughness, they would have understood each
other better. As it was, you could not argue with Nellie;
she just let you have your head. Martha had found that
hard to handle. Everyone had thought Nellie Phelan
was perfect and it was hard to live with perfection, or
at least she had found it so.

Was Peter like herself? She knew that Jack thought
so. He had never said it, but then Jack could let you
know these things without saying a word. But even if
Peter was like her, Jack could still see enough Phelan
in him to understand him. As for Jack and herself,
there would never be the understanding that he had
with Kate and Nora, but still they had a healthy respect
for each other. The fact that she had looked after
Mossgrove well was an important factor in Jack's eyes.
He loved the land above all.

She looked again at the photograph: Ned and herself twenty-two years ago. They looked so young and
happy! She looked at her own face, far more beautiful
than it was today, but at the same time a face that had
done very little living. *Just as well*, she thought, *that we
cannot see down the road ahead of us. That view would certainly have wiped the smile off my face.*

Martha had come out of a very different home from
Mossgrove. Her father was withdrawn and silent and
did not encourage callers, so the easy comings and
goings of Mossgrove had been very hard to take, and

she had discouraged them from the beginning. That had not gone down well with the neighbours.

Nellie Phelan and Jack were like a guard of honour around Ned, who could do no wrong; Martha felt that she was on approval and that, in their eyes, she never quite measured up. She had found it a difficult situation, and the only way she could handle it was to push them all away from Ned and herself. Ned was often confused by her attitude, but she had her own ways of bringing him into line. Peter, however, was a different kettle of fish and opposed her on all fronts. He was not going to be forced into doing anything that was not his own choice.

She heard Peter's door bang and then the soft thud of his stockinged feet along the corridor and the usual creak of the third step of the stairs. Jack would have the cows in by now, and Davy would be arriving with a head full of sleep and protestation. Like Ned, getting up in the morning posed no problem for Peter, but Nora was the sleepyhead who hung in there until the last minute.

Martha got out of bed, thinking as she dressed of all she needed to do before they caught the bus to Ross. It would have been handy if Kate had offered a lift as it would have spared so much time. The fact that Kate was in the dark about the will had made a big difference. Old Hobbs had really cleared the air on that one. Of course, he would not put himself out very much to help herself.

She was setting the table for the breakfast when she heard a car in the yard and looking out the window saw Kate's Morris Minor. When she did not come in straightaway, Martha knew that she had called up to the stalls to Jack and the boys, but a few minutes later she came into the kitchen ahead of them. Kate's smiling face had always irritated Martha and no less this morning. How on earth could you have anything to smile about at this hour of the morning?

"Martha, would you like a lift to Ross later on?" Kate asked tentatively. "It would be no bother, but if you'd prefer to be on your own I could understand that, too."

Why did Kate always have to be pussyfooting around her?

"It would suit us fine to get a lift," Martha told her.

"That's grand, so I'll be here around two," Kate said, disappearing out the door and colliding with Peter.

"What's the hurry?" he demanded. "Why don't you stay and have a cup of tea with us, or weren't you asked?"

"I was actually," she lied, "but I'm in a bit of a rush. I'll be back later on to take you all to Ross."

"Oh, good," he said, "you'll be there for the unveiling of the past."

"No, no," she told him hurriedly. "I'm only chauffeuring."

"Well, then, you'll get the news hot off the press," he told her.

When Kate had gone, Martha decided to take

advantage of these few minutes alone with Peter before Jack and Davy came in. She would probably have no other opportunity before they visited Hobbs.

"Peter, whatever happens today, I would like you to know that whatever I did in the past I was doing the best that I could at the time," she said with difficulty.

"Well, Mother Martha," he said, "you're the one who is always complaining about Aunty Kate going around in circles and now you're at it."

"Forget it," she snapped at him, annoyed that he would make no effort to meet her halfway.

"What's wrong with you?" he demanded. "Are you afraid that today Nana Nellie will be back to haunt you? She'd have good reason, but she won't bother, because life is probably more peaceful where she is."

"You're impossible," she told him and was glad when Jack and Davy came in the door.

"How's you mother, Davy?" she asked without thinking and saw the surprise in his face that she bothered to enquire.

"Wouldn't you call back to see her?" Peter cut in before Davy had a chance to open his mouth.

"Oh, she's shagged," Davy told her, ignoring Peter. "She was the one that was always up yowling around the house at the crack of dawn to get us out of bed. She was worse than Jack here in the morning. Now she wouldn't care if we died inside in it. I used to be stone mad with her for dragging me out of it so early, but I declare to God, now I'd be glad of it."

"It will just take time," she told him, and decided that she would go to see Ellen Shine during the week. At least she had some idea what the poor wretch was going through.

The mealtimes in Mossgrove were set in concrete: breakfast after the morning milking, dinner at one o'clock, tea at four o'clock and supper after evening milking. It had to be something important to change the dinnertime, but today Martha brought it forward to twelve in order to avoid rushing to get ready for Ross. She hated rushing; it was the one point of argument between Nora and herself. Nora was a last-minute person who never seemed to have heard of hurry. Wherever they were going, they all finished up waiting for Nora. Today was no different.

Peter stood at the foot of the stairs yelling up at her, "Norry, it's not to a dance you're going, so what is all the doing up for? I doubt that Old Hobbs is going to be swept off his feet."

"You've no sense of occasion, Peter Phelan," his sister informed him loftily, coming down the stairs at a leisurely pace. "We are going to see the family solicitor about something that could change the whole course of our lives, so we need to be dressed accordingly."

"Baloney," Peter told her. "He probably has some minute legal details to straighten out, and we'll be rushed in and out like going to the dentist."

Fine for him to be so relaxed, Martha thought. She was feeling tense about the whole thing.

"Come on, for God's sake, will ye?" Peter urged. "Kate is outside talking to Jack with the last ten minutes."

"Is this skirt all right, Peter?" Nora asked, twirling around, and Martha knew that she was just winding him up. They did it to each other all the time.

"I'm going," he declared and banged the door after him.

"My brother has no patience," Nora decided. "Come on, Mom, or we'll be walking after them."

Out in the yard Peter was in the front of the car with Kate, who was giving him elementary driving instructions. Martha and Nora sat into the back and as Kate drove out of the yard, Jack waved them off.

"We should get a car," Peter declared.

"You must learn to drive first," Nora told him.

"A piece of cake," he assured her.

"I'd probably learn faster than you," Nora said, "because I wouldn't get excited so easily."

"Norry, you'd never get started," Peter told her.

"Did you never hear the story of the hare and the tortoise?" Nora demanded.

"But even the tortoise moved."

She lent forward and gave him a smart slap on the back of the head and he ducked sideways, expecting another one.

"Be careful, Pete," Kate warned, "or we'll all finish up in the ditch."

Martha was only half hearing what was going on. She

wished that this interview was behind her and whatever the outcome, she could deal with it then. The waiting and not knowing were a strain.

During the entire journey, Nora and Peter kept up a stream of chat with Kate, almost forgetting about Martha, which suited her. When they arrived outside the office, Kate parked and turned back to Martha.

"Will we all meet in the hotel across the road in an hour's time?" she suggested. "We'll have tea together, and if you're all there before me, go ahead and I'll join you when I'm finished. I've a few things to do."

Martha knew that she was giving them time to sort themselves out before she joined them.

"Oh, that will be just lovely," Nora declared, before her mother had a chance to voice an opinion.

"Not so slow now, Norry," Peter teased.

"Stay quiet," Nora ordered. "I love having tea out. There is something very posh about it."

"God help you."

When they went into Mr Hobbs' waiting room, Peter and Nora looked around curiously.

"Mark would have a great time in here," Peter decided, looking around at all the bare walls.

"Shush," Nora whispered fiercely when the secretary looked disapprovingly over her spectacles at them. "This is probably the way these kind of places are supposed to look."

"Depress the clients before you get them in," Peter suggested.

"Peter, you have an opinion on everything," Nora told him scornfully, "even things that you know absolutely nothing about."

They sat on a hard timber bench opposite a door through which the secretary had disappeared. When she returned, she held the door open.

"Mr Hobbs will see you now," she informed them, and they trooped in.

Mr Hobbs placed his gold-framed spectacles on the polished desk and uncoiled his thin length from behind it. He came forward and shook hands formally with the three of them.

"You sit here, Mrs Phelan," he said, indicating Martha to an upright armchair in front of his desk. "And now, Miss Phelan, would you like to sit here?" He put a straightbacked chair on Martha's left. "And you here, Mr Phelan," and Peter was seated on her right.

Now that we are all to his satisfaction, he will start to play God, Martha thought.

"Thank you for coming," he began courteously, which Martha thought a bit unnecessary because after all they did not have much choice.

"Are you all quite comfortable?" he asked, and she felt like shouting, *Will you for God's sake get on with it.* But Mr Hobbs was in no hurry. He drew the green file, the only thing on his desk, toward him and carefully drew out the yellow document. Martha felt as if he were opening the lid of Nellie Phelan's coffin. Hobbs would be doing the reading, but it would be her voice speaking.

A slight shiver ran up her spine. Peter looked at her peculiarly and she pulled herself together.

"Now, Mr Phelan," Mr Hobbs began in his silken voice, "I believe that you will soon be twenty-one, coming of age, so to speak." He smiled thinly.

"That's right," Peter told him.

"Well," Mr Hobbs continued, unfolding the document and ironing it out on the desk with the side of his long, thin hand, "we won't go into all the legal details, but in essence what is relevant at the moment is that this will states that if either of your parents had died before you attained you majority, you would then become a partner with the other in the farm known as Mossgrove."

There was absolute silence in the room. Martha could hardly believe what she was hearing. Peter a partner in Mossgrove! He would be impossible. It just could not work. They could never work it out between them. Her mouth had gone dry and she could feel her head thumping. She became aware that Peter was speaking.

"What exactly does that mean?" he was asking in a shaky voice.

"Exactly what it says. You will be party to all decisions. Your mother cannot act without your consent and you cannot act without hers. That applies to all management and working decisions on the farm. Now, as regards the financial side of things, both your names will go on to the Mossgrove bank account."

195

There would be no new house. She heard Mr Hobbs voice from a long way off.

"And now for you, Miss Phelan," Hobbs continued, smiling at Nora who smiled back uncertainly, not quite sure of all the implications unfolding around her, "you will have right-of-residency in Mossgrove until you decide to marry. If you never marry, it will continue for life."

"What is right-of-residency?" she ventured.

"The right to live there," he said.

"But, sure, of course she'll have that," Peter broke in indignantly.

"Of course," Hobbs said agreeably, "but it has another implication. Mr Phelan, should you ever decide to sell Mossgrove, she could prevent it."

"That won't arise," Peter told him shortly.

"Glad to hear it," Mr Hobbs told him.

Martha's mind snapped back into alertness. Now it would come out about Kate's objecting to the sale of Mossgrove, and whatever hope herself and Peter had of working together would be blown away for ever. She could see Peter straining to take in all the implications, and with his next question she held her breath.

"When Nana Nellie left the farm to Dad, did she make the same arrangements?" he asked.

It would be important for Peter that he was being treated the same as his father. *Now*, she thought, *he is going to find out!*

Then to her amazement she heard Old Hobbs say,

"Your aunt had a very good job when you father died and could support herself."

It was not a lie, simply an evasion of the truth. She looked at him in amazement, and he returned her gaze with an expressionless face and then smiled vaguely at the three of them.

"Will we get a copy of the will?" Peter asked.

"You know, Mr Phelan, sometimes wills are like life and it is better to deal with them when the relevant events unfold," he said evenly, and Martha knew that they would not get a copy and for that she was grateful. But Peter was still in search of details.

"But what if my mother and I run into difficulties?" he persisted.

"And that may be a possibility," Hobbs told him, and Martha felt that he had the situation well sized up.

"More than a possibility," Peter assured him.

"Well, in that event, we have two executors, Mr Jack Tobin and Mrs Sarah Jones, both lifelong trusted friends of your grandmother's. They will see that the will is administered fairly," he told them.

Martha's feelings were in disarray. What she had dreaded most had not happened, but the will had presented her with another problem. What was it that Jack used to say? That worries are often overcome by events. It had just happened.

Mr Hobbs was rising to his feet, letting them know that the interview was coming to a close.

"Your minds are probably reeling with unasked

questions," he told them, "but maybe it is better to go home and get used to things and then come back at a later date if you want another discussion. In the meantime, I will be sending you the relevant details and will be writing to Mr Tobin and Mrs Jones."

He shook hands politely with each one of them and they left his office in a bemused state.

When they gathered around the table in the Ross Arms, Nora, the only one to have recovered her equilibrium, was ordering fancy cakes and gooey pastries with gusto. Martha was silent and Peter seemed uncertain as to what was expected of him. Finally he blurted out, "I'm simply floored by that."

"Can you imagine how I feel?" Martha snapped.

"Well, I suppose you could say that the playing pitch is level anyway," he suggested.

"With two referees: Jack and Sarah," Nora chirped in.

"Both of them on your side," Martha told Peter.

"I'd say that Jack won't be on either side, only Mossgrove's," he said, "and Sarah will agree with Jack."

"So Mossgrove is the winner," Martha said.

"Won't everyone be surprised?" Nora said, but Martha cut in, "There is one thing I want to say to the two of you now, not a word about this to anybody. We will keep it to ourselves for a while."

"But why?" they chorused.

"I have my reasons," she told them.

CHAPTER SIXTEEN

DANNY CONWAY WATCHED his father stride down the field and rest his arms on the stake over Yalla Hole. Matt Conway never tired of staring across the river. The sight of the black burned rings, his sign of victory over the Phelans, seemed to give him immense satisfaction.

His father had been in a dreadful temper after Fr Brady's sermon and his mother had a black eye to prove it. When he came home and saw the state of her, Danny had been sorry that he had stayed on to play the match. He should have anticipated that there would be a backlash. If he had been at home, he could have taken the brunt of it, but he had been so carried away by the game that he forgot.

Playing in goal as he did, it would not have been easy to miss the final, and once the game got started there was no time to think of anything else. It was great to have Davy Shine in front of you, because very little got past Davy. If Davy thought that he might not be able to block the ball, he shouted back instructions. Between them they had saved Kilmeen in many a nail-biting finish, and if ever anything got past them, Davy always shouldered the responsibility with him.

Davy was a good friend, but Danny was always cautious around Peter. He felt that Peter blamed him for his father's carry-on. Nora on the other hand was always friendly. She had been like that even when they were going to school. If there was a fight between the big boys, he and she often hid behind a ditch until it was over.

He had started writing to Kitty and Mary and went to Sarah Jones' to collect the reply every week. She was such a kind person, and it was just so good to be catching up on the girls' news. Imagine having a flat all to themselves in Dublin. Some day he was going to visit them.

Matt Conway turned and walked up the field, as Danny watched him through the broken window of the pigs' house. He had followed his father everywhere since the burning of the hay. It was only a matter of time before he struck again, and Danny wanted to be there to stop him. He had stood outside the door the night that his father had threatened Jack Tobin, hoping that Jack would use his shotgun.

The thing that worried Danny most was that his

father had now taken to hiding below the path that the Phelans used to take a short cut back to Lehanes'. The first day his father had let Martha Phelan see him, but since then he had remained hidden. He watched Martha and Nora, and Danny watched him. If his father was out in the haggard, he could see Martha or Nora leaving their own yard, and then he went down and crossed the river and came up through the wood and hid below the path.

In recent days it was only Nora he went to spy on, mostly late in the evening when she went back to see her grandmother. It worried Danny sick in case he might do something dreadful. On a few occasions he was tempted to confide in Sarah Jones, but he was too ashamed to tell her. Maybe he was only imagining it and his father had no notion of doing anything only spy on them. But why was it only Nora that he watched now?

Soon after his father saw her leaving Mossgrove, he would leave the haggard, and Danny would follow him at a safe distance. He wondered what he could do if anything happened, because his father was as strong as a horse and could easily get the better of him, so he hid a hurley under a bush just beyond where his father stood watching the path. Hopefully he would never have to use it, but if he had to he would need the element of surprise.

Now his father came into the house where he was feeding the pigs.

"Are you finished there yet?" he demanded.

"Nearly," he said quietly

"You weren't worth rearing," his father told him, walking amongst the pigs and kicking them squealing out of his way. Danny continued pouring the meal into the trough and then went out to bring in another bucket. Mostly he could ignore his father's aggression when it was directed only at himself.

"What's wrong with you lately?" his father demanded. "You haven't a word to throw at a dog."

"Nothing," Danny answered.

"I'll give you more than nothing if you don't straighten yourself up and get a bit of a move on around the place," his father threatened.

Danny was tired because, when the old fellow often got up at night to ramble around the fields, he followed him, and then afterwards he could not get to sleep because he had his ears strained listening for movement. Being an unseen bodyguard to his father was draining his energy. His mother knew that he was following him, but Danny did not want to worry her by giving her any details. She had enough to put up with, and if she knew nothing he could beat nothing out of her. It did not seem so long ago since she had been shielding him. Living with his father was like living with a time bomb.

Today there was a suppressed excitement about Matt that worried Danny. He was like a volcano, about to erupt and do something crazy. Danny could not leave his father out of his sight, especially at the time that Nora went along the path. Usually she came home before the cows were driven out after milking in Mossgrove because she got the supper ready for the rest of them.

That evening when his father brought their own cows in early for milking, Danny became more uneasy. It looked as if his father was planning to be finished earlier than Mossgrove. Could it be just a coincidence or had he some ulterior motive? His father and mother milked silently, each moving between their own cows, and he too had his allotted ones. When they were all finished, he drove the cows up into the field behind the house. When he came down, his father was not in the haggard or yard, and when he checked the kitchen, he was not there either.

"Did he come in?" he asked his mother.

"No. What's wrong, Danny?" she asked.

"Nothing, I'll be back later," he said hurriedly.

He walked carefully down through the back field, keeping in by the ditch until he reached the river further upstream from Yalla Hole. Part of the river was shallow here so he crossed easily until he came to the deep water, where he had to balance himself carefully as he walked along the plank his father had thrown across to the far bank. He was glad to get into the shelter of the wood where he could not be seen. Following the winding path that climbed upwards, he drew near his father's hiding place and slowed, moving silently from tree to tree. If a twig cracked beneath his foot, he was in trouble. He hid for a few minutes behind a large tree with tufts of ivy hanging off the trunk. Without being seen he could see through the ivy. At first he thought that there was nobody there and started to breathe more easily, but then a slight movement caught his eye. He watched steadily for a few minutes and saw that his father was hiding in a cluster of bushes just beside the path.

Danny moved quietly to the piece of raised ground where he had hidden the hurley. He could hear his heart thumping with fear. Now he had no doubt but that his father intended to do something. *Dear God!* he thought, *I should have told Sarah Jones. It's all my fault and now it's too late to do anything.* But maybe Nora had not gone to her grandmother's; she didn't go every evening. But the old fellow wouldn't be here if he had not seen her walking back.

From where Danny was hiding, he could oversee the path and his father. His only chance was to wait and move at just the right minute and catch the old fellow off guard. Otherwise his father would get away with whatever he had in mind and lay himself out as well. His heart was thumping so loud that he felt it could be heard all over the wood, but his father never moved.

Maybe she would not come or her Uncle Mark would be with her. If that would only happen, he would go straight to Sarah Jones and tell her the whole story. *Dear God, give me that chance,* he prayed. She was seldom this late and he was just beginning to breathe easy when he heard her singing. He could feel his throat tighten and his mouth go dry. She was walking along the path picking wild woodbine and sniffing it as she sang happily to herself. Her yellow dress was the same colour as her bunch of woodbine. She snapped off a piece with a long stem and pushed it into her blond hair, where it settled in a nest of green leaves. As she passed beside him, she was smiling happily and he recognised her song as "The Young Ones". They had danced to it in the village a few weeks ago. She gave a little twirl along the path to the rhythm of her singing. Then she was right in front of where his father was hidden. Danny could feel the blood thumping in his head. To his horror, she reached up to pluck an overhanging bunch of woodbine, and his father's hand shot out and caught her wrist. Danny could see the stunned look on her face as she opened her mouth to scream, but his father was out on the path with his hand over her mouth and the scream turned into a stifled gurgle.

"Take it easy now, little girl, and nobody will get hurt." His father voice came hoarsely up to Danny.

Nora's eyes were dilated with terror as she flailed with her hands and legs. His father was able to hold her with one arm while he pulled a dirty rag out of his pocket and rammed it into her mouth.

"Now, Miss Phelan, we'll see who's boss here," and catching the yellow dress he ripped it down the front.

Danny's vision blurred with terror, but he could not move. He had to wait until his father was more at a disadvantage. If he moved too soon and got it wrong, he would be useless. Nora was hysterical, belting out with her arms and legs, but she was powerless against such brute strength. His father threw her on the ground and put his boot on top of her to keep her there while he grappled with the buckle of his belt. He swung his belt free, tossed it into the briars, and then went down on his knees straddling Nora, who reached up and clawed his face. Danny moved down silently with the hurley in his hand. Nora was dragging at his father's hair and his father was thumping her with his fists. Now was the time. Danny crashed the hurley down on his father's skull and he toppled sideways on to the path. Danny dragged Nora to her feet and whipped the rag out of her mouth.

"Run," he shouted.

She stood staring at him with a glazed look in her eyes, and he could hear his father grunting behind him. She was rooted to the ground.

"Nora, Nora," he shouted shaking her, "will you run, for God's sake, run!" He faced her for Mossgrove and gave her a push, and then she was running, a lop-sided shunting run, as if her co-ordination were gone askew. Her torn dress dragged behind her. He turned to find his father clambering to his knees with blood streaming down his face.

CHAPTER SEVENTEEN

As Peter and Davy arrived into the kitchen, Jack was laying the table and Martha making the tea.

"Where's Norry?" Peter asked in surprise, drying his hands and throwing the towel over the banister.

"It's not like her not to have the supper ready," Martha said in a puzzled tone of voice. "I wonder what delayed her?"

"Well, Norry is never in a hurry," Peter smiled. "All the time in the world . . ."

"Still," Jack interrupted, "she always has the supper on the table."

"I'll go and see what's delaying her so," Peter decided, going towards the door.

As he opened the door the sound of screaming cut like a razor into the quietness of the kitchen.

"Jesus Christ, what's that?" Jack gasped as the screams drew nearer.

"Oh my God!" Davy breathed, staring wide-eyed at the door.

"It can't be. . ." Peter began.

"Oh no! Oh no!" Martha gasped, running towards the door, "don't let it be Norry. Norry, it's Norry! Oh mother of divine God, it's Norry!"

Peter was clung to the floor, but Martha rushed past him and caught Nora as she stumbled in. Blood pouring from her nose was staining the front of her torn dress and splashing red on her bare skin. Briars clung to her hair and tattered clothes. Her piercing screams filled the kitchen. Jack, feeling the strength leave his legs, grasped the nearest chair and whispered to himself, "Conway."

"Oh my God," Martha gasped, wrapping her arms around Nora.

"Oh Mom, Mom, Mom," she yelled. "Peter, Peter, Peter."

"Norry, what happened?" Peter gasped, but his voice was drowned.

"You're all right now," Martha soothed, holding her close. "You're all right, you're safe, you're safe."

Nora's arms were like vice grips. Martha's stomach locked in spasm and panic gurgled at the back of her throat, but she held the hysterical Nora firmly. The others watched with horror etched on their faces. Jack sat on a chair, holding the ends of the table.

"Lift her on to the couch with me," Martha instructed Peter.

"Jesus! She's all black and blue," Peter whispered as Nora's torn dress fell away to reveal dark bruises beneath tattered underwear.

"What happened to you, Norry?" Peter whispered, forcing the words out between clenched teeth.

"Matt Conway," she sobbed.

"Matt Conway! Oh, Jesus Christ!" Peter groaned, burying his face in his hands. Then he straightened up and strode for the stairs.

"Where're you going?" Martha demanded.

"Dad's gun," he muttered in a choked voice.

"Jack," Martha ordered, "hold Nora," and in two long strides she was across the kitchen, confronting Peter at the foot of the stairs. She caught him by the shoulders and shook him.

"Peter, just now it's only Norry who counts. Forget Conway; he's for later. It's Norry now and only Norry. Go for Kate this minute and, Davy, you go for Sarah Jones. I want those two women here straightaway. We must take care of Norry now."

"Your mother is right," a white-faced Davy intervened. "We'll go for the women."

When they had left, Martha covered Nora with a warm blanket.

"We'll wait for Kate and Sarah," she said, "before we move her any further."

Nora was moaning quietly now as she lay cuddled up

on the couch with Jack's arms around her.

Martha strode up and down the kitchen, her mind raging. Why had she let this happen to Norry? She alone was responsible. Why in God's name had she not put a stop to him before now? Peter and Davy had wanted something done, and she alone had held off. This was all her fault. She should have carried out her plan. *Oh, but I am going to do it now. By God, is he going to pay!* She felt her stomach churning and rushed to the sink in the back kitchen. When she raised her head, the back kitchen swung around her and cold perspiration ran down her face. This was the most shocking thing that had ever happened to them. It was worse than Ned's death. At least death was clean. What had that animal done to Norry? She couldn't even bear to think about it. Then she straightened her shoulders, wiped her face with the towel and came back into the kitchen. Jack looked at her in concern with an unasked question on his face and she nodded her head.

"Are you all right, Mom?" Nora whispered.

"I'm fine," Martha assured her, "and you'll be fine too. When Kate comes we'll clean you up and put you to bed."

"I don't want to be alone," Nora whispered, tears running down her face.

"You won't be alone," Martha assured her.

She looked at Jack and Nora together on the couch. He was rubbing her hands and hair and humming their own little tune with which he had lulled her to sleep years ago. He was trying to comfort and calm her as if she were a child again. Martha had seen him do it many times to injured farm animals. Nora reached out her hand and touched his face.

Martha felt the soothing wisdom of this old man. His face was grey with shock, but he was still able to pull himself together and ease Nora with his healing touch. Martha sat on the couch with them and tears spilled down her face. It was the first time that Jack had ever seen her cry.

Kate was the first to arrive and slipped silently into the kitchen. She talked gently to Nora as she peeled off the torn clothes.

"Thank God, she's here," Martha whispered to Jack as he went quietly out the back door.

"Martha, fill the bath with warm water and pour in some of this," Kate said, handing Martha a bottle.

"You'll be all right, Norry," Kate soothed her. "There is nothing broken and all the bruises will fade."

"But I'm so cold and frightened," Nora sobbed, her teeth chattering.

"You'll soon warm up in the bath," Kate comforted her as she eased Nora's panty down over her slim legs and asked gently, "Are you sore here?" Kate queried gently.

"No, Danny came and hit him with a hurley," Nora told her.

"Thank God for Danny," Kate sighed. "I'll slip this towel around you and we'll make it to the bath."

Nora winced as she straightened up, but with the help of Kate and Martha she climbed the stairs. Martha was relieved to have Kate with her, and by the time Sarah Jones came Nora was in the bath. Kate washed her face and hair and gently cleaned off the dirt and leaves. As they were drying her, Martha asked, "Do you want to go into your own bed, Norry, or come down to the sofa?"

"The sofa," Nora said. "I don't want to be alone."

"Sarah, will you fix up the sofa, and I'll go out to the two boys, in case they'd do something that will land them in trouble."

When Nora was settled comfortably on the sofa, Kate handed her two tablets and held a glass of water to her lips.

"Take these now, Norry, and they'll make you sleep and take away some of the soreness."

"If I fall asleep, you'll still be here, Aunty Kate?"

"I'll be here," Kate promised.

A few minutes afterwards they knew by her deep breathing that she had gone to sleep.

"She's not going to get over this in a hurry," Sarah whispered.

"No," Kate agreed, "it will leave its mark, but only for Danny it could be worse."

"Danny will come to me and we'll find out the whole story. It might be a while before Nora comes out with it," Sarah said. "Will Martha report it to the Guards, do you think?"

"I doubt it," Kate said. "She didn't report the hay burning, though they came around asking questions."

"He must be stopped," Sarah decided. "The man is out of control. What will he do next?"

Out in the yard Martha found Jack leaning on the gate staring across the river at Conways'. She joined him and they both looked over silently.

"If it could only have been me instead of Norry," Martha said. "She is only a child. I can't bear to even think of it."

"He must be stopped," Jack said quietly.

"He will be stopped," Martha told him with determination.

Jack looked at her. "You have a plan?" he asked quietly.

"I have."

"I thought you had since the night in the meadow."

"You don't need to know, Jack," she told him. "Tomorrow morning I want you to go in and order that tractor that Peter and Davy have been eyeing in Kelly's Garage."

Jack looked at her in astonishment, and she knew that he was wondering how on earth a tractor came into her plan. She had no intention of burdening him with details.

"Nobody is to know. Instruct Kelly that we will tell him the exact day we want it delivered."

"You have your reasons, Martha," Jack said quietly.

"I have my reasons, Jack."

CHAPTER EIGHTEEN

D ANNY DIVED INTO the wood and tore through the undergrowth, not looking where he was going. At first he thought that his father was behind him, but after a while he realised that it was his own crashing sound and the terror thumping in his head that he was hearing. He lost track of time and kept running until he fell into a dyke exhausted. His teeth started to chatter and sweat ran down his forehead. Nora's distorted face swam in front of his eyes. Would she ever get over it? He was used to violence, but she was reared in a loving home. Apart from her mother and brother, Jack and Davy doted on her. She had her grandmother and Uncle Mark and her Aunty Kate, and she was treasured by all of them. Violence had never raised its ugly head in her world. Why did this have to happen to her now?

Then he thought of Mary and Kitty and what they had gone through, and it came to him with blinding clarity that he would kill his father. It was the only solution to the whole problem. He did not know when or how he would do it, but he would work it out and do it. He could finish up in prison, but what were they living in now but a prison? His mother had been a prisoner all her life. She deserved some years of freedom. Once the decision was made, he felt a great sense of freedom. He stretched out in the dyke exhausted.

He had no idea how long he had been asleep, but when he woke the sky was full of glittering stars and a full moon was looking over the hedge. There was absolute silence, and when he moved a surprised bird fluttered out of a bush beside him. Stiff with cold, he straightened up and felt the dew on his shirt. Where was he? He had run blindly, noticing nothing. He looked for a familiar landmark. Walking around the field he found a gap, went through two more fields, and then he saw the school up on the hill. Now he knew where he was, but there was no way that he could go home. He thought about it for a while and then decided that he would go to Sarah Jones.

Since the conversation with his mother, he had become a frequent caller to Sarah and had found her helpful and comforting. She seemed to know everything that was to be known about his family, so he felt at ease with her. Nothing surprised Sarah. The chances were that she had already been down to Mossgrove, so she would know about Nora. What a fool he had been not to have told Sarah about his suspicions. He could have stopped the whole thing and spared Nora a terrible ordeal. He'd never forgive himself for that.

Suddenly he stumbled over a stone, and when he put his hand up to steady himself, he was startled that his fingers touched wood beneath the briars instead of the stone ditch. The moon came from behind a cloud and he found himself looking through the briars at a narrow plank that could be covering a gap in the ditch. Moving back the growth, he eased the plank sideways and stepped down into a small square opening. There could be no doubt but that this was his grandmother's still for making the cure. All the signs were here. His grandmother was dead with years, but it was obvious that it was still being used. Who knew about this little hideaway and was continuing to make the cure? Then he noticed a cap hanging off one of the churns. It was Jack's. So Jack was in operation here on the quiet. Had he been in on it with his grandmother or had he picked up where she left off? Danny backed out and slid the plank back after him. He would never have seen it but for stumbling against it. It might be a good place to hide if he ever needed it.

When he knocked at Sarah's door, there was no movement for a few seconds. Then he saw the curtains being edged back and Sarah's face in the shadows of the bedroom. He heard the bolt being pulled and the door opened.

"Come in, Danny," she whispered. "I was expecting you."

The sight of her comforting face and the warmth of her welcome was such a relief that his self-control cracked. When she seated him into her comfortable armchair, great sobs shook his body.

"You've had a terrible night," she soothed him, "and it's good to cry."

"You know about it?" he asked.

"I do. I was below."

"How's Nora?"

"Shocked, of course, and we were glad when she fell asleep. Kate is down there for the night, so she'll look after things."

"I feel so guilty," he told her.

"But only for you, Danny, it could have been much worse," she assured him. "Tell me exactly what happened."

So he told her from the beginning, leaving out no detail and blaming himself for not having told her of his suspicions.

"Danny, my dear," she told him, "we're all wise after the event. You did what you could and at least now we know exactly what happened. It would be very hard on Nora to be questioning her about the details and expecting her to go back over it so soon."

"How are the rest of them?" he asked fearfully.

"Peter and Davy nearly went berserk and Martha had to stop them from taking Ned's gun after your father."

"God, it's what he deserves," Danny said.

"Then they'd be in trouble," Sarah told him. "That would only make the story worse."

"I'm going to sort it out," Danny told her with determination.

"Don't do anything stupid," Sarah warned.

"He's not fit to be alive. My mother has had a terrible life with him."

"It won't improve her life if you finish up in jail," Sarah stated. "You're all she's got at home with her now."

"If he was gone she'd have some kind of a life," Danny declared.

"Not if you are not there," Sarah told him. "She's used to him, but it would kill her altogether if anything happened to you."

"We're trapped, aren't we?" Danny said sadly.

"Maybe this time your father has taken a step too far," Sarah said quietly.

"Did Martha send for the Guards?"

"No."

"Is she going to do nothing?" he demanded in desperation.

"I doubt it," Sarah said.

The following morning as they had their breakfast together, they discussed a plan of action.

"You can't go home," Sarah warned him. "He'll kill you."

"But I can't stay hiding here either," Danny told her.

219

"He could burn you out."

"Well, you can for a while anyway," she told him, "until we see what way the wind is blowing. When he's gone to the creamery, I'll slip over to your mother and tell her that you're all right."

"I wonder how's his head? I gave him a fair belt of the hurley."

"Your father has a head like a mallet," Sarah told him. "I've seen him come out of fights that would have killed an ordinary man."

"You're right," Danny agreed. "He's probably going on this morning as if nothing happened yesterday. He's as strong as a bloody ox."

"The best thing you can do now, while you are stuck in here with time on you hands," Sarah instructed, "is sit down and write to Kitty and Mary. They are delighted that you are writing to them now."

"God, 'twill be hard to write without mentioning last night," Danny said.

"Well, don't! What they don't know won't bother them," Sarah assured him.

"Do you know who's making the cure now?" he asked her suddenly, remembering last night.

"I do," she answered. "Do you?"

"I found out last night," he told her.

"You discover strange things wandering around by night," she observed.

"If the old fellow discovers that I'm here, I'll hide there," he told her. "He doesn't know about it, does he?"

"No," she assured him.

"It's a real safe corner away down at the bottom of the glen," he said.

"I'll pass on the word that you might be using it."

CHAPTER NINETEEN

THE NIGHT CREPT by on leaden feet. To move too early would be courting disaster. After days of careful consideration, Martha had decided that 2.30am would be the best time to make her move. Any earlier and there could be somebody still around; any later the early summer dawn would catch her out before she was finished.

Every time she looked at the little alarm clock on the bedside table, she thought that the hands should have moved further on. She even checked it against her watch with the light of a flashlamp under the bedclothes. It was safer not to turn on the light; she wanted nothing to draw attention to the fact that she was awake that could be remembered afterwards. It was vital to keep things looking normal. There was too much at stake to overlook the smallest thing.

At last the clock hands reached the appointed time. She slipped out of bed and rumpled the bedclothes to give the appearance that there was somebody still in it, just in case Nora looked in. For a few nights after the attack, Nora had slept in Martha's bed before feeling able to go back to her own room, but one night since she had come in during the night. If Nora thought that she were asleep, though, she might let her be.

The clothes that she planned to wear were neatly folded in the bottom of the wardrobe. Removing her nightdress, she pushed it under the bedclothes and put on her underclothes. Then she stepped into an old black pants of Ned's and tied it firmly around her waist and slipped a long black jumper over her head. She folded the ends of the pants firmly around her ankles and eased a pair of long black socks up over them. Catching her long black hair, she whipped it into a knot at the back of her head and pulled a cap of Ned's down over it. At a distance now she could be mistaken for a man.

As she picked up a pair of boots, she glanced back at her wedding picture on the wall.

She closed the door quietly and went softly down the stairs, skipping the creaking third step. Sitting at the bottom of the stairs, she carefully laced her boots. Feeling her way around by the walls of the kitchen, she was guided by the red glow of the Sacred Heart light. Taking the bits of meat that she had already prepared, she stuffed them into her pocket. Wagging his tail,

Bran met her outside the back door. She held the door open to let him in and closed it firmly after her. The last thing she wanted was Bran following her.

The little trowel and wire pincers were where she had hidden them, behind the water barrel. It was so dark that she had to feel her way around, but this was what she needed. She had waited for a night such as this, watching the sky and judging its suitability. On a bright moonlit night she could be seen from an over-looking window in the valley. Tonight was dark with no stars.

Keeping close to the wall, she went across the back-yard and up through the haggard and along the little boreen into the Moss field. She walked by the hedge down through the three fields to the river. Either the night was getting brighter or else her eyes were grow-ing accustomed to the darkness. She prayed that the moon would not come out.

She knew exactly where the shallow part of the river was, beyond Yalla Hole. It was as if the river, having gone to the depths, was then content to run along the surface. As she came out of the shadows into the open, she forced herself to move slowly. It only took her a few seconds to cross the ferny patch to the river but it seemed like eternity. With her head down she crouched as low as possible. The big stepping stones were well clear of the water after all the dry weather. Conway had once tried to dig out the stones, but they were so embedded with time that there was no shifting them. It was a long stride from one stone to the other as the dark water swirled around her feet. Almost slipping off the last stone, she clung to the long grass on the opposite side.

She clambered up the bank. Now she was on Conway land, dangerous ground. Going down on her hands and knees, she crawled along the bank, and gradually it curved upwards and arched out over Yalla Hole. She would have to crawl under the wire to get to the other side and reach the spot where Matt Conway always stood looking across the river at them.

Keeping very still, she listened for a sound that would tell her if there was movement up in Conways' yard or if the dogs were around. Their farmyard was two fields up from the river, but the dogs sometimes hunted at night. Her fingers encircled the bits of meat in her pocket. She knew that once she went under that wire there would be no escape. Drawing a deep breath, she gritted her teeth. Lifting up the wire, she eased her head and shoulders under it and then, sagging her back down, she dragged her legs after her. She was on the other side now. The grass was smooth under her hands as she crept along until she reached a hollow beside one of the stakes. This was Matt Conway's spot. She listened carefully for any sound, but there was only silence.

She began to dig around the base of the stake. The ground was hard, dried out by the summer sun, and perspiration ran down her forehead. She had to blink it out of her eyes and it tasted salty on her lips. Gradually a little pile of earth rose as the hole around the stake deepened. Suddenly she froze. There was movement behind her. She clenched her teeth to stop them from chattering, her heart pounded and there was a thumping in her head. After a few seconds she forced her rigid neck to turn and looked behind her. She could see nothing there, but it was so dark that there could be somebody quite close and she would not see them. Maybe somebody was waiting in the darkness. *Calm down*, she told herself, *and keep going.* A few more scoops and she would be at the base of the fencing post.

When she reached the bottom of the post she loosened the earth all around it, then filled the hole very loosely. What was she going to do with the surplus earth? When she had thought this out at home, she had planned to ease it over the bank into the river. Now she was afraid of the noise it might make, but she had no choice. Very gently she eased it slowly over the bank and was relieved when the trickle-down was barely audible. With her hands she dusted the grass completely clean of the brown earth and covered the ground around the post with the top sod that she had first cut away. Now the stake had no grip. If anyone leant against it, only the wire could still hold them.

Her heart was thumping and the perspiration was running down her back, partly from the frantic digging, but also from sheer terror. Terrible pictures flew across

227

her mind of what would happen if Matt Conway caught her, and she had to take a grip on herself to keep from running down the bank and back across the river. It was tempting, but Nora's terrified face swam in front of her eyes. He was going to pay for what he did. If she did not finish what she had come to do, she would regret it. She had never run away from anything in her life.

There were two strands of thorny wire going from this post to the ones further along the bank. She knew that it was rusty old wire by the rough feel of it, and the brown wool she had in her pocket would look the same. Winding the wool around the little cluster of spikes just beside the stake, she tied it to the wire at the other side. It had to be strong enough to hold the stake in position. Then she did the same with the lower strand. All the knotting was at the river side of the stake.

Working carefully, she was conscious that time was slipping by and that soon the dawn would be breaking. It had all taken longer than she had planned. Now for the real test. Cutting the wire very slowly with the pincers, she held her breath. The wool stretched but held; unless you looked very carefully you would not notice the difference. She breathed a sigh of relief. Suddenly dogs barked up in Conways' yard. She froze to the ground. *Move*, she told herself, *and get under the wire.* Her body was stiff with cold and tension. She was halfway under the wire when she remembered the trowel and had to reverse back and grab it. The rusty spike of wire dug into her hand, but she hardly felt it.

She clambered down the bank on all fours, taking cover in the rushes and high ferns. When she reached the river, she was afraid to stand upright, so she crawled across, the water soaking in through her clothes. The dogs had stopped barking. When she reached the opposite bank, she reached upwards to grasp the long grass and caught something cold and slippery that squealed. She choked a scream and slipped back into the water with a loud splash. The dogs started barking again in Conways'. She clambered up the bank, almost blinded by fright, and crawled until she got to the shelter of their own hedge. Then she straighted up and looked back at Yalla Hole. There was somebody standing in the shadows just beside the stake, looking across at her. She blinked quickly to make sure that it was not her imagination playing tricks, and then there was nobody there. Her nerves were so strained that she was seeing things!

For a few seconds she stood rooted to the ground, too frightened to move. Matt Conway could easily be here at this side of the river, lying in wait for her. At least with her back to the high ditch he could not creep up on her, but she would have to move. When she heard a faint cough she almost fainted and then was flooded with relief when one of the horses snorted in the darkness. She moved quickly then and almost ran along in the shadow of the hedge. Light was spilling into the centre of the fields. There had been just enough time.

Carefully she opened the back door. Bran wagged his tail and was delighted when a shower of meat pieces came after him into the yard. The relief of being back in the safety of her own house was intense, though she was still shaking with cold and fear. She breathed deeply to ease herself of tension. It was the first time in her life that she had tasted terror. The warmth of the kitchen embraced her, and she stood in front of the Aga to peel off her wet clothes. The cold was gone into the marrow of her bone, and her muscles were ice-stiff. She bundled up the wet clothes and pushed them to the back of the press; she pulled out a big towel to rub herself dry and to get the heat back into her body. Opening the two doors of the cooker to better warm herself, she pulled a nightdress out of the press and put it on.

Gradually she thawed out, but she knew that it would be a long time before her mind would recover from the tension of the night. A glass of Jack's cure would be the best thing for her, so she put on the kettle and waited for it to boil.

Jack's bottle was up in the parlour, and when she opened the door old Edward Phelan met her eyes across the room. She felt he would have understood what she had done tonight.

CHAPTER TWENTY

ANNY WATCHED SOMEBODY walk close to the hedge, keeping well into the shadows. It was a dull night and he could only barely see the outline moving slowly along. The person must have come down from Mossgrove, and Danny was puzzled as to who he was. He did not walk like Peter, was too thin to be Davy and too tall to be Jack. Whoever he was, he was taking great pains not to be seen. Danny watched him from beneath the hedge just above Yalla Hole. He had come over from Sarah's under the shadow of dark to check on one of the calves who had been a bit shaky on his legs. His father took very little care of sick animals.

The stranger walked towards the river. Danny was surprised when he crossed the river using the stepping stones, nearly slipping off the last one, and then crawled up the cliff over Yalla Hole. Danny held his breath when the stranger passed so close that he could have put out his hand and touched him. What on earth was he up to? It was only when he started to dig and a long strand of hair came down under his cap that it dawned on him who it was: Martha. He got such a shock that he had to smother a gasp. He froze when she stopped digging, turned her head around and looked in his direction. For one awful moment he thought that she had seen him, but then she returned to her digging and it struck him that he was invisible in the dark shadows.

What on earth was she doing? Then slowly the understanding of what she was at dawned on him.

As she crawled away, he thought that she had forgotten the trowel, but then he saw her retrieve it. He watched her crawl across the river and then slip back down into the water when she started to clamber up the bank. The long grass that she was using to haul herself up must have given way. Then she was on the river bank and heading for the shelter of the hedge. As she stepped into the shadows and turned and looked back, his heart almost stopped. She was looking directly at him. In his anxiety he must have stepped out of the shadows; now he quickly slipped back. He could see her outline beside the ditch and wondered why she was standing there. Suddenly she moved and walked quickly along by the hedge, and then she disappeared deeper into the shadows and remained hidden all the way up to Mossgrove.

Danny stared at the stake. He wanted to walk away and go back up to Sarah's or Jack's still, but something held him. He felt that he had to stay. It would be too dangerous to remain at their own side of the river, however, because if the dogs came down they would sniff him out. It would be better to cross over to the Phelan side and wait there in the trees from where he had sight of Mossgrove, their own place and the cliff above Yalla Hole. Crawling out of the bushes, he followed Martha's path across the river, but then turned into the sheltering trees where he settled down in the high grass. It would be a long wait.

As the first cracks of light appeared in the darkness, the dawn chorus began in the wood behind him. It was his first time really listening to it. It began gently and very slowly, the volume increasing until the whole wood seemed to be singing. The only one he had ever heard talking about the dawn chorus was Nora. When she was a child, Jack used to call her some summer mornings to hear it. At the time he had thought it was a bit strange but now he was not so sure. It was the grandest sound that he had ever heard.

Suddenly tears came into his eyes as the beauty of the birds' singing and the shock of the whole situation overcame him. He knew then that he would never have had the courage to do anything to his father, and even sitting here now waiting for something to happen was unnerving him. Should he let it happen? Even now he could save his father. Then Nora's face swam in front of him and he remembered his mother over the years. No, he would just sit here and let things go ahead. If Martha Phelan could do it, then he was not going to interfere.

The morning dragged on, and as the hours went by his stomach churned. When the sun rose in the sky it became very hot and his mouth dried with thirst, but he dared not leave the shelter of the trees. Too restless to stay in the one position, he stretched out on the high grass and looked up at the sky through the trees. It was strange to be spending so much time in the one corner doing nothing. He had never been in a quiet corner like this for so long. The hard knot of anxiety in his stomach grew tighter.

Then suddenly he heard the buzz of an engine coming from Mossgrove. He crawled along and looked out from behind a tree. There was a tractor coming down the fields, a new one. It must have only just arrived, and Peter was testing his driving skills under Jack's and Davy's supervision. There was a lot of yelling and shouting, with Davy running ahead directing Peter.

There was no doubt but that this would bring his father down to his lookout point. Danny waited with his eyes screwed to their own haggard, and sure enough his father appeared, stood staring across and then strode down the field. Even from where he sat, Danny knew that his father was in a temper. The sight of a new tractor in Phelans' was enough to do that. Striding towards the fence, his attention was concentrated on

Mossgrove. Danny wanted to look away, but his eyes were glued to the stake in horrified fascination. His throat tightened and a cold sweat broke out on his forehead. His father leant forward towards the stake. Danny's brain went into slow motion.

A blood-curdling bellow came across the river. He was never sure afterwards if he had really seen it happen or if his vision had been too blurred. One minute his father was there on top of the cliff and then that terrible sound and he was gone. Was he in Yalla Hole or could he be clinging to the sides? If he had not fallen straight down, he could have landed near the bank and be dragging himself out. Danny did not move. If his father was trying to pull himself out of the river, he did not want to be there.

Then he heard shouting. The men in the field had seen it happen and were running down to the river. Peter was ahead with Davy after him and Jack bringing up the rear. Danny watched them reach the bank where they stood looking into the river without moving. He knew then that his father was nowhere to be seen. He must have gone straight down into Yalla Hole. Danny's stomach was churning and vomit gurgled up his throat. He sank to his knees and let it pour on to the grass.

As Danny came slowly out from beneath the shelter of the trees and climbed down the bank towards the river, Davy was the first to hear the rustling of the rushes behind them. When he turned, his normally cheery face was pale with shock.

"He fell in over the cliff," Davy said in a stunned voice. "The bloody stake must have been pure rotten."

"Did you see it?" Peter asked Danny in a strained whisper.

"I'm not sure," Danny said hesitantly. "One minute he was there and the next he was gone."

"It all happened in the blink of an eye," Jack said quietly. "Nothing comes up out of Yalla Hole."

They all stood staring into the river as if the water had the answer to what had just happened.

"What are we going to do, Jack?" Davy asked eventually.

"You will have to go up and tell your mother, Danny," Jack said gently, "and Peter, you and Davy had better go to the village and tell the Guards."

"Why the Guards?" Danny asked.

"An accident," Jack explained to him, "has to be reported."

Danny stood there for a long time rooted to the spot. He felt that to move was to set in motion a train of events that he might not be able to handle. The others stood waiting for him to be sufficiently recovered to go up to tell his mother. He closed his eyes and the whole picture replayed itself again in his mind. Then he felt Jack's hand on his shoulder.

"Would you like me to come up to your mother with you, lad?" he asked.

"I don't know," Danny stammered.

"I'll walk up with you anyway and then you can see," Jack told him.

As soon as himself and Jack started to cross the river, Davy and Peter headed up the fields to Mossgrove. Danny walked along the edge of the cliff until he came to the gap in the wire. The stake had taken a lump of the earth before it into the river. Nobody would ever know that it had previously been dug. He picked up the ends of the wire lying on the grass. The rusted wire could have simply cracked from pressure. Unknotting the bits of brown wool, he put them into his pocket. Jack never said a word.

Danny's mother was sitting at the table having a cup of tea when he came into the kitchen. Her face lit up when she saw him.

"Danny, I've been so worried about you." Then she stopped and looked at him. "You look terrible."

"Mam," he began, sitting on a chair beside her, "something has happened," and he stopped. What was the best way to put it?

"What?" she asked anxiously.

"Dad is in Yalla Hole," he blurted out bluntly.

"Danny," she screamed, catching him by the arms, "you didn't push him in?"

"No, no," he assured her, "the wire cracked and he fell."

"Oh, thank God you weren't the cause of it," she gasped, closing her eyes. She kept them closed for so long that Danny began to wonder if she had gone into some kind of a faint. When she opened them she said simply, "I would have wished him time to make peace with his maker."

The two of them sat in silence and then his mother said, "He had no peace here. Maybe he'll find it where he's gone."

"We hadn't much peace either," Danny said.

"No," she agreed, "but the place will take a lot of getting used to without him."

"It's hard to imagine it," Danny said.

"I suppose the rest of them will have to be told," his mother said vaguely.

Danny saw that she was not going to be able to make any decisions and that it was up to him to decide what to do. His mind was so confused that he did not know where to begin, and then he thought of Jack waiting outside in the yard. Jack would know how to handle things.

"You go in to Jim in the post office," Jack told him, "and get him to send off telegrams to the lads, and I'll go for Sarah and Agnes. Women are always better in these situations."

Danny went into the kitchen where his mother was still sitting in the same place staring into space. "Mam, the old notebook with the addresses in it, where is it?"

She looked at him blankly, so he rooted through the drawer in the press that held all sorts of odds and ends, but the little dog-eared notebook was not there. He searched another drawer. *Where the hell is it? These bloody drawers are always in such a mess, you can never find anything in them.* Then his mother stood beside him and reached in behind a large dish in the dresser and handed him the little red notebook.

"You have Mary's address in your head, haven't you?" she asked, and when he nodded she returned to the chair.

God, how did she think of where the notebook was and a few minutes before she couldn't even hear me!

"Will you be all right, Mam," he asked, "while I'm in the village?" She made no attempt to answer him, and he went out into the yard to see if there was any trace of Sarah coming. He had better lock up the dogs as they weren't used to strangers around the place. Yesterday he could not have made that decision; his father always had them running loose to frighten people away.

As he was bolting the door, Sarah cycled into the yard.

"Danny, child, I'm glad that you're all right. When you were missing this morning, I was half worried about you," she said, getting off her bike. Danny wondered what she must be thinking when he was missing half the night, but she never asked a question.

"When you're in the village, call to Kate Phelan and she'll be able to ring Mary later on," was all she said.

The news had reached the village before him. After his call to the post office, where Jim knew exactly what to do, he called to Kate Phelan.

"Danny, you've had a terrible shock," she said calmly, drawing him into the front room.

"Sarah Jones said you would ring Mary," Danny told her.

"I will and I'm sure she'll be here tomorrow. It will be good for your mother to have herself and Kitty come quickly."

"I can't believe it," Danny said simply.

"That's understandable." Kate looked at him closely. "When did you eat last?"

"Yesterday, I think," he told her.

"Well, that won't keep you standing," she told him. "Come into the kitchen and we'll have something to eat."

As he was leaving the room, the picture over the mantelpiece caught his eye. He stood looking at it.

"That's my grandfather," Kate told him quietly.

"Edward Phelan," he said reflectively. "The story goes back to him and my great-grandfather, doesn't it?"

"I believe so," Kate said.

It was a strange feeling to be looking into the face of the man who had been there at the beginning of all the trouble. How his father had hated the memory of this man. He looked at Kate. As a child he had always associated her with taking Kitty away. Now he knew the truth.

"You were friends with my grandmother," he said.

"We understood each other," Kate told him.

"She was good to us," Danny said.

"She was a strong woman."

When he got back home, the neighbours had gathered. The men stood around the yard in groups talking quietly, and when he came into the yard they came forward to shake his hand. He was glad when Davy came out of the barn and they sat on a wall under a tree at the side of the yard. There was something reassuring about Davy.

"God, 'tis murdering hot, isn't it?" Davy declared, wiping sweat off his forehead.

"We haven't seen rain for weeks," Danny said.

"It's coming, though, I'd say." Davy looked up at the hazy sky. "It's so bloody hot there's a thunderstorm coming. That sky is full of rain to the west."

"Did you see him fall?" Danny blurted out.

"The odd bloody thing is," Davy declared, "that I'm not sure. We saw him tearing down the field, and then the next thing he was at the stake, and then the stake seemed to tilt forward and down. It was all over before you could say cush to a duck."

"Do you think that he'll come up?" Danny asked.

"They say nothing comes out of Yalla Hole," Davy said, "but then you don't know."

"Will the Guards drag it?" Danny asked.

"Doubtful," Davy decided. "There's a pile of shit down there, dead cows and donkeys and everything."

"'Twould be easier if we had a funeral," Danny said.

"It might," Davy agreed. "There is something tidied up about a funeral."

"It would be better to have him in the graveyard than so near us in Yalla Hole," Danny said.

"I see what you mean," Davy agreed.

The day dragged on and Danny was glad when it was time to milk the cows. It was good to be doing something normal. Davy stayed to help, and as they milked Danny found himself telling him what life had been like with his father. Davy listened and when Danny finished advised, "It's good to tell it as it was, but, Danny, now he's dead you'll have to let go of all that stuff or 'twill poison you."

As they crossed the yard after milking, they heard the first crack of thunder and lightning streaked across the darkening sky.

"We're going to have a deluge," Danny declared, running for the shelter of the barn.

It rained all night. Danny listened as it banged off the iron roof. Some of the neighbours stayed and the kettle boiled endlessly for cups of tea and hot cure. In the morning Davy came back to milk the cows. Afterwards he and Danny walked down to the river. They stood on top of the cliff and looked down over the flooded inches. The brown water was swirling out over the banks and the body of Matt Conway was wedged between the stepping stones beyond Yalla Hole.

CHAPTER TWENTY-ONE

I T WAS THE day of Matt Conway's funeral. Martha
knew that she would have to go because her
absence would be the cause of comment.

Over the years, she had watched him lean on that
stake and had wished that it would give way under his
weight, and the thought of helping it along had ger-
minated on the night of the hay burning. She had hesitated to take the final step, but when Nora had come
home on that terrible night the decision was made.

That night had changed all their lives. Nora's exu-
berance was gone and she went around the house like
a shadow. She had lost her glow, as if a light had been
extinguished inside. Peter had lost his work drive, and
Martha knew that the damage to Nora was harder for
him to bear than if something had happened to himself. It had aged Jack in a way that no amount of work

would ever have done, and Davy was quiet and subdued. That night had hurt them in a way that nothing before had ever done. Martha had decided then that a final stop would have to be put to Matt Conway.

Watching Nora move around the house like a grey shadow had torn the heart out of Martha. To even think of what had happened to her was hard to bear, but she found her mind constantly dwelling on it. The visit to Mr Hobbs paled into insignificance. The running of Mossgrove was of no consequence compared to what had happened to Nora. She understood Peter's desperation about it, and for the first time they had a common bond with no friction.

She had given Jack very precise instructions about the delivery of the tractor. Matt Conway had to be brought down that field the morning after the weakening of the stake. The new tractor would be the bait that would bring him there. She could not take the chance of one of the cows using the stake as a scratching pole and spoiling her plan. Jack would wonder afterwards, but he could always be relied on to keep his own counsel.

The entire scheme had unfolded as planned, and now it was all over. What had to be done had to be done, and she would do it again if she had to. The man was a threat to all of them. Getting the Guards in on it would have been a waste of time. Over the years she had seen him get away with all kinds of thuggery because he was too smart to get caught. Well, this time he had gone a step too far. If only she could heal Nora and bring back the daughter who had been like sunshine around Mossgrove.

Kate was collecting them for the funeral. At first Nora had decided that she did not want to go but then changed her mind. Martha would have been as happy if she had decided to stay at home but let her decide for herself. It was difficult to know what would be the best thing for her. Kate was of the opinion that maybe it would be best if she were there. If Nora stayed at home, Peter was going to stay with her, and if she went he would go too. In the end it was decided that they would all go together.

Martha dressed carefully, wearing her black leather gloves in order to cover the deep scratch in her hand. She had seen Jack looking at it one morning, and when Peter had remarked on it, she had dismissed it lightly as something that happened when she was searching for hens that were nesting outside. She had a feeling that Jack was not convinced. It would be healed in a few days and she wanted as few people as possible to notice it. When she was dressed she went along to Nora's room and found her sitting on the bed staring out the window.

"Come on, Norry, and get dressed if you're coming," Martha said gently.

"I'm not sure that I can face it," Nora whispered. "Any funeral I was at I was sorry that someone was dead, but this time I'm not, and maybe that's wrong."

"Very few will be sorry after Matt Conway," Martha assured her, "even his own family, I'd say."

"I'd forgotten about them," Nora said regretfully. "It is a terrible day for them because he was awful to them. When Dada died we were all so sad and maybe that's easier, is it, than this way?"

"I don't know," Martha told her, "but however they feel they will have to put up with it."

"You are very strong, Mom," Nora told her. "You would probably have got the better of Matt Conway that night. I seemed to have been paralysed with fear. Only for Danny he would have done horrible things to me. The thought of it terrifies me."

"Well, he didn't," Martha said firmly, "and once today is over, we'll put it behind us. He has taken our peace of mind for long enough."

When all this was over, it might be good to take Nora away somewhere. They would have to work something out. It would be good for the two of them to get away for a while.

"I'll get dressed so," Nora said, "and I'll be down in a minute."

"I doubt it," Peter said, appearing at the door. "Your minutes are fairly long, Norry." Martha was glad to see the ghost of a smile on Nora's face.

"We'll see which of us will be in the kitchen first so," she challenged Peter.

"You're on," he told her, running back to his own room.

Half an hour later they were in Kate's car heading for the village.

"We'll all sit together in the church," Kate suggested.

"Like Brown's cows," Peter told her.

"Whoever Brown was," Kate smiled.

Kate found it difficult to find a parking space near the church. Bicycles were lying along by the railings while pony-and-traps and cars lined the street at both sides of the church. Martha maintained that even if the devil were dead a crowd would gather to bury him in Kilmeen.

"You're a great fellow when you're dead, aren't you?" Peter said wryly.

They looked in the back door but the main aisle seemed to be packed up along, so Kate said, "We'll go around to the side aisle. There's always room there."

The side aisle just beside the altar was almost full as well, but Kate poked out four seats near the top. They were not far from the altar and the Conways were straight across from them. Martha would have preferred to be nearer to the door and not in such close proximity to the Conways.

After a while she looked across at the Conways. Biddy was miserable-looking, as usual. Rory and Tom were like the father, big and burly, and Danny, the odd man out, tall and slim. But it was the girls who really caught her attention. Mary was dark and elegant, with her hair coiled into a knot at the back of her head. Martha remembered her as a small, black, snotty little thing. The years had certainly brought about a big change. It was hard to believe that Biddy and Matt Conway had produced someone like her. But if Mary was a surprise, she was in the shadow compared to Kitty. Martha decided that this had to be the real ugly duckling story. The Kitty she recalled had been thin, wizened and foxy. Now she was tall and slim with a mass of red hair streaming down around an elfin face. She heard Peter's intake of breath beside her when he recognised Kitty and she felt like putting her hand over his and saying, "Don't even think about her, because we have had enough trouble with Conways already and we're going to be finished with them after today."

Then Nora leant over and whispered to her, "Isn't Kitty simply gorgeous?"

"She is," Peter agreed from her other side.

It was the strangest funeral mass that Martha had ever attended. Everyone was unsure if they should be sorry or glad for the Conways. If they were totally honest, they could only be relieved he was dead. There were all sorts of rumours as to why those girls had had to leave home, and if only the half of them were true, they had no reason to mourn their father. Martha thought of Matt Conway in the glossy coffin and decided that it was the safest place for him. In there he could no longer harm anyone.

The entire congregation rose to their feet when Fr Burke, in purple vestments, swept on to the altar flanked by a retinue of altar boys. His booming voice filled the church and they were swept along on the tide of ritual. *There is a lot to be said for a ritual,* Martha considered, *because it carries us over uneven patches that we might not be able to manoeuvre left to ourselves.*

She tried to remember Ned's funeral mass, but it was a hazy nightmare of grief and despair. That was eight years ago and now the children were grown up, and maybe it was time to give Peter his head. Jack might be right, that he had the makings of a good farmer. After all, young Danny Conway would be running the place across the river now and he was younger than Peter. Danny would surely get the place, although looking across at Rory Conway she was not so sure.

Then Fr Burke began his sermon. The Conways sat with bowed heads. *Surely,* Martha thought, *he will not be stupid enough to dish up his usual drivel about a great loss to the family and parish.* She wondered how she would handle it if she was giving the sermon. Probably the one about throwing the first stone might be the best bet. Then she realised that Fr Burke was in full flight, heaping praise on Matt Conway to such an extent that Martha decided that you could be forgiven for thinking that you were at the wrong funeral.

What is the bloody man thinking of? Has he any idea what is going on in his parish, or is he trying to turn Matt Conway into a saint before our eyes?

Martha stole a glance at the Conways. All heads were bowed except for Mary, who was gazing at Fr Burke in disbelief. Suddenly she rose to her feet. She was sitting half-way along the seat, so she had to pass by some of the others to get out. Martha saw Rory try to stop her, but there was no stopping this tall, dark, determined girl. It was only when she came out of the seat that Fr Burke and the rest of the congregation became aware of her. She walked purposefully towards her father's coffin and faced Fr Burke on the altar. He stopped short in mid-sentence and a ripple went through the congregation. Then there was absolute silence in the church. She placed her hand on her father's coffin and began to speak in a clear, calm voice.

"I do not know where my father is today, but I hope that it is in a more honest place than we are in." She spoke very slowly and each word winged around the silent church as she continued. "He was neither a good husband nor father, and I do not want him to be buried in a shroud of lies. He was the way he was, and just because he is dead he cannot be turned into someone else. We will try to forgive him for the way he treated us, and I think that it would be easier if we buried him with honesty."

She returned to her seat and Fr Burke stood looking after her with a stunned look on his face. *Hopefully,* Martha thought, *he will have the good sense to keep his mouth shut and continue with the mass.* He had.

Martha looked across at Mary Conway in admiration. That had taken great nerve. The old grandmother was supposed to have been a remarkable woman.

Mary had obviously inherited some of her guts. She certainly did not get it from Biddy.

After mass the Conway boys came forward to shoulder the coffin down the church. There was a brief moment of confusion when there was no one for the fourth corner of the coffin, but before it became a problem, Davy Shine stepped forward and stood in with the boys.

"Isn't Davy kind?" Nora whispered to her.

Martha nodded wordlessly, thinking that if Davy was thinking along her lines, he had decided that the quicker Matt Conway was under ground the better.

The Conway grave was in the furthest corner of the graveyard behind the church. The crowd gathered around the open grave as Fr Burke splashed the coffin with holy water and said the prayers for the dead. When it came to the prayers for the bereaved, he hesitated slightly but went ahead. As the first sods hit the coffin, Martha took Nora's hand, and she knew Kate was at her other side with Peter behind them. *How would they feel*, Martha wondered, *if they knew the truth, that I brought this day about with careful planning?* She was glad that they would never know, because it would probably upset them far more than she was going to allow it to upset her.

Afterwards they went to shake hands with the Conways. Kitty was nearest to them and her face lit up with delight when she saw Nora.

"You look so different, Nora," Kitty told her, holding

on to her hand. "I hardly knew you."

"So do you," Peter assured her.

"Peter," Kitty gasped. "You're a young man."

"Well, I'm twenty," Peter told her. "I should be."

"You've all grown up since you met last," Martha told them, "but we'd better move on as we're holding up the queue."

"Kitty, when are you going back?" Nora wanted to know as she was moved on

"I'm not sure," she called after Nora, "but couldn't we meet?"

"I'll fix something up," Kate told them as Martha moved on to shake hands with Mary.

"You're a girl of great courage," Martha told her.

"I needed it, Mrs Phelan," Mary told her quietly, looking her straight in the eye.

This is the one, Martha thought, *who is going to sort out this lot and get things moving again.* As she shook hands with Rory Conway she decided that he was the one who was going to give her most trouble.

Afterwards back in Mossgrove they sat around the table and discussed the funeral.

"Well, I suppose any one of us wouldn't like to say that he was great stowing," Davy proclaimed.

"Well, Mary put no tooth in it," Peter declared.

"I never in my life saw the likes of that at a funeral," Jack told them.

"She's taking after the old lady," Kate told them. "You remember her, Jack. She was like steel."

"A mighty old warrior," Jack agreed, shaking his head at the memory of her.

"Isn't Kitty just lovely? Why did she go away after her grandmother died?" Nora asked.

There was a moment's silence, and then Kate said evenly, "To keep Mary company, I think," and Martha thought, *Like hell she did.*

"Well, she looks so lovely now that I would hardly know her," Nora said in an impressed voice, and Martha realised that it was best that she had gone to the funeral. Martha decided she would ask Kate to tell Nora the truth about Kitty and Mary later, and it would probably put things into perspective. But now was not the time.

"I wonder what will happen across the river?" Davy said thoughtfully.

"You were very kind, Davy," Nora told him, "to go under the coffin."

"It was time to move him on and I was sorry for poor Danny," Davy told her. "The other two are right old shaggers, especially that Rory."

"The girls turned out the best," Kate concurred.

"God, Kitty is a smasher," Peter declared.

"You keep your eyes off her, young fellow," Davy advised good humouredly. "We've had enough Conway trouble in this house, so don't you be drawing any more on us."

Amen to that, Martha thought.

As the conversation continued around the table,

Martha decided that this was as good a time as any to tell the rest of them about Peter's becoming a partner in Mossgrove. It would distract them from the Matt Conway business. She tapped her cup with her spoon and all eyes swung toward her.

"I have something to tell you all," she began. "Some of you know that Peter, Nora and myself went to see Mr Hobbs about two weeks ago or, to put it more correctly, we were summoned to meet him. Well, the result of the meeting was a surprise which we told nobody until now. Peter and Nora wanted to tell you all straightaway, but I asked them not to, as I wanted to get used to the idea. When I heard the news first, I admit that it came as a bit of a shock, but subsequent events have changed my priorities. As you know, Peter will be twenty-one shortly. . ."

"And ready to act the big man," Davy interjected.

"Davy, will you ever shut up," Peter told him.

"Well, according to Nellie Phelan's will," Martha continued, "when Peter becomes twenty-one, his name is to go on the deeds of Mossgrove with mine."

There was a chorus of exclamations from around the table.

"The new boss," Davy declared.

"Not quite," Martha said evenly; "a joint effort."

"Well, that's great news," Jack said in delight. "No chance of heading for the gate now, lad. My old bones will rest easier."

"Congratulations, Peter," Kate said warmly. "You will be a great help to your mother."

"Now, young fellow," Davy advised, "don't you go getting notions above your station, just because your name is going on a bit of paper in Old Hobbs' office."

"Oh, I'll crack the whip now, slave," Peter assured him, clapping Davy on the back. "You're in for. . ."

"One minute now," Jack interrupted, rising to his feet. "We must salute the occasion."

"Oh, Jack," Davy protested, "yourself and your bloody cure."

"The wine of Kilmeen must be drunk to mark this auspicious event," Jack declared, striding for the parlour and returning with a bottle marked "holy water".

"Martha, girlie, get the hot water and some glasses," he ordered. It was a measure of how carried away by the occasion he was that he called her "girlie", his term for Kate and Nora. *I must be coming up in his world,* she thought wryly as she poured the hot water into a jug.

"Jack has a great sense of occasion," Kate declared.

"You might call it that," Davy told her, "because he judges you sufficiently mature in years to partake, but Peter, Nora and I will be on lemonade."

"I like lemonade," Nora told him.

"That's blind loyalty for you," Davy told her.

"Let's get on with it," Martha instructed, arriving with the steaming jug, and Jack began the ritual of measuring and adding and mixing. When the three glasses were to his satisfaction, he handed them around with a flourish.

"And lemonade for the children, Martha," he told her, going to the parlour for another bottle.

"Children!" Peter and Davy chorused in protest.

But there was no stopping Jack as he splashed lemonade into heavy tumblers.

"Now, let's drink a toast to Mossgrove," he declared, "and to the great people who kept it going over the years, and to Peter who is going to do us all proud in the days ahead."

They all stood and raised their glasses: "To Peter."

CHAPTER TWENTY-TWO

F̱R TIM LOOKED at his fishing rod and thought longingly of the river, but it was Saturday night and he had confessions at eight o'clock. He knew that David would be already down on the river bank, waiting expectantly for the little tug at the end of the line and the excitement of reeling in a wriggling brown trout. *There is a lot to be said for teaching,* he thought, *no late evening confessions, no sick calls and fine long holidays.* But then he smiled as he remembered his mother saying, "Bloom where you're planted." *So now, Tim,* he told himself, *head down for the church and bloom for an hour in the musty confessional.*

When he reached the church, he was not surprised to find that he had two seats full of people and Fr Burke had half a seat. That was the usual Saturday night procedure. There was need to toughen up a bit in order to reduce the odds. Sometimes he heard Fr Burke growling across the aisle, and he wondered what on earth was the man hoping to achieve. Life was difficult enough for people, and most of them were trying to do the best that they could.

The little timber grid shunted back and forth rhythmically as, one after another, people thrust their heads in under the green felt curtain. The usual Saturday rituals poured forth: stealing, lying, backbiting and an occasional uncontrolled passion. Through the split in his green baize curtain, he saw Fr Burke leave his box. Tim sometimes wished that he would move more quietly. Since his visit to the bishop, Tim had bent over backwards not to cross swords with him and had been amazed at how tranquil life had become once he became determined to keep his head down and his mouth shut.

It was with relief that he heard the last penitent leave the box. He had pulled the stole from around his neck and had his hand on the door to push it open when he heard someone come in at the other side. He sighed. It was most likely a man with a drink problem, hoping for the strength to give it up and not wanting to be seen by anyone. He would probably have to draw back from the strong breath of alcoholic vapours that would assail his nostrils.

It was strange how tuned his nose had become in the close confines of the box. Before people began, he was fairly sure of their age and sex. Children, though enclosed in strict confines, were all movement, most men were poised for exit and some women thought that he had all day and that there was no one outside waiting to come in after them. If this was a drunk, the chances were that he was in no hurry and wanted someone to listen to his wronged life story.

But when he slid back the grid he was surprised to get a feminine whiff of perfumed soap. She began in a businesslike voice: "Bless me, Father, for I have sinned, a month since my last confession."

"Yes?" he said encouragingly, sensing that this was not run-of-the-mill.

"I am not sure whether this is a sin or not, but I decided to come to confession anyway, just in case," she told him.

"Let's see," he said quietly.

"I took certain steps to help Matt Conway fall into Yalla Hole and drown," she told him, and he recognised with a start who was at the other side. What on earth did she mean? *Take it easy now, Brady,* he told himself, *and handle this very carefully.*

"What do you mean by certain steps?" he asked.

In a matter-of-fact voice she filled him in with all the details, not blaming herself or lessening her involvement either. Tim felt that he was getting it exactly as it had happened.

"You did this," he asked her, "because he burned the hay?"

"No," she told him. "I thought about it after he had

burned the hay. Then one night as Nora was coming from her grandmother's, he attacked her and would have done terrible things to her if Danny had not been following him. So I decided then that I'd put a stop to his gallop."

That is one way of putting it, he thought. How come it had never dawned on anyone that it could have been anything other than an accident? Of course, Guard O'Keeffe would not have bothered drawing any complications on himself, and the thought had never crossed anyone else's mind. Well, it was done now, and himself and Martha would have to sort out this end of it as best they could.

"Are you sorry for having done this?" he asked.

"I'm sorry that I had to do it," she told him.

He decided that if he were to go into things any deeper he might drown in deep theological waters.

"The best that we can do is pray for him," he told her, "so say the rosary for the repose of his soul."

As she said her act of contrition, he said the words of absolution, not quite sure if they had all the required ingredients in this particular confession, but feeling that it was probably as good as they could do in the circumstances.

Just as she was about to leave the box, Martha turned back and said, "It took courage to give that sermon about the hay. Thank you," which surprised him, because from his experience of her she was not given to too many words of praise or appreciation.

"How is Nora now?" he asked.

"Not herself, but if I could get her away from here for a while, it would probably do her good."

"And yourself as well," he told her.

"You might be right," she agreed, and then she was gone as quietly as she had come.

What an extraordinary woman! He sat in the box to give himself time to recover from the shock. It was his first confession of murder. But was it murder? It was certainly sailing pretty close to the wind, but then on the other hand it might not have happened. *It's too complicated to sort it out,* he thought, *and what good would it do anyway?* She was lucky that she did not have a finely tuned conscience, because afterwards it might come back to haunt her. But Martha was tough enough to handle it.

When he came out of the box, he thought at first that the church was empty, and then he saw somebody by the back door. He was about to walk up the church when he saw that it was Danny Conway, looking a bit bothered.

"Are you all right, Danny?" he asked, walking back towards him.

"I'm not sure, Father," Danny told him uncertainly.

"Come into the sacristy and we'll chat it out," Tim told him.

"Maybe I should go to confession," Danny said hesitantly.

"We can do that in there too if needs be," Tim assured him.

After a few hesitant starts, Danny told his story. *This is like a jigsaw puzzle,* Tim thought, *all the pieces falling into place.* Martha would have been amazed if she had known that she had been under observation, and from what Danny was saying it would not surprise him if Jack had an idea of what had happened. If Jack was able to piece it together, then Kate would have it, and that might be a good thing. They would be able to support Martha even though she would be unaware that it was happening. Strange how things worked out.

Danny was feeling far more upset than Martha, and Tim did the best he could to reassure him that he was blameless. After confession they sat down again and discussed it in greater detail. Then Danny felt the need to go back over the years with his father and Tim listened. *If I was not burdened with my priestly conscience,* Tim thought, *I would be deciding that Martha had done them all a good turn.* When Danny finally came to the end of his story, Tim told him, "Try to leave it behind you now, Danny, or it will ruin the rest of your life."

"Davy Shine said the same thing," Danny told him, "but it's easier said than done."

"Davy was right, but any time you want to talk, I'm here to listen," Tim promised. "What's happening about the farm?"

"Mary thinks that they should all sign off their claim and give it to Mom and me, but Rory is being awkward," Danny told him.

"Would I be any help?" Tim asked.

"Afraid not, Father," Danny said regretfully. "He'd listen better to Fr Burke."

"I'll have a word with him," Tim said, remembering the bishop's words about some people having great time for Fr Burke. *It takes all kinds*, he decided, *and we are all here.*

Later as he walked down the street to his own house, he thought what a strange few weeks it had been in the parish. All the revelations attached to Matt Conway's death were startling. Feeling in the need of fresh air, he decided that he would get out his rod and go down to the river. The light was fading, but David might still be below there. Looking down the street, he saw Rodney Jackson's long car parked in front of their house.

He was just pulling his waders out from the press under the stairs when the doorbell rang.

"Blast it anyway," he protested. "Is there no end to them?"

When he opened the door, he was very surprised to see Rodney Jackson on the doorstep. The lean American towered over him and the tanned face that was normally smiling was looking slightly strained. Tim had often met him down at Kate and David's, but he would not have thought that they were on visiting terms. *But then*, he thought, *everyone is on visiting terms with you in my job.*

"Fr Brady, I hesitate to intrude on your privacy," the American drawled, "but I do need a little advice."

I must be a lot smarter than I thought, Tim decided, *if this high-powered businessman is coming to me for advice.*

"You're very welcome, Rodney," he assured him, opening back the door and leading him into the sitting room and at the same time thinking of the fish that were going to live a day longer.

"As you know, Father, I would not be familiar with the way things are done in Ireland," Rodney Jackson began, and Tim, thinking of the hour just gone by, considered that that might be no bad thing.

"You find it different from America," Tim suggested.

"In some ways," the American said. "Now, I like the way you handle things over here in your ordinary day-to-day living, but beyond that I would be walking in the dark."

A bit like I am right now, Tim thought. *What on earth is the man getting at?*

"This may be a bit out of line, Father, but I have no one else to ask, and the priest usually knows the correct procedure in most things," Rodney Jackson said.

"I'll be glad to help in any way I can," Tim offered, wondering what was coming next.

"As you know, I've been coming here regularly for the last eight years. During that time, I have been very impressed with a certain lady, but I am at a loss as to how to proceed, as you may handle these things differently here, and I want to do this correctly from the beginning."

By God, Tim thought, *but he's coming to the right man for*

264

advice. If he wanted to find someone clueless in that department in the parish, he could not have made a better choice.

"You see, Father," Rodney Jackson continued, "the problem is that this lady already has responsibilities and I'm not quite sure how to make my approach."

Who can he be talking about? Tim wondered. *It is surely not Kate, but then who else does he know?*

"Who are we talking about here?" Tim asked tentatively.

"Oh, I beg your pardon," Rodney Jackson exclaimed. "I should have stated that in the first place. A lady you know well."

This cannot be happening to me, Tim thought, and waited.

"Martha Phelan," the American informed him, "a most wonderful woman. I only know her through Mark, but I have been more impressed with every meeting. She is such a refined lady."

Tim swallowed hard and struggled to keep the look of astonishment off his face, but must not have succeeded.

"You are surprised, Father?" Rodney Jackson asked.

"Well it's a bit unexpected," Tim admitted hurriedly.

"You see my dilemma, Father," Rodney told him. "If you are that surprised, how would she feel? Then there's Mark and Agnes and her children. I would not like to upset anybody or have them think that I was taking advantage of Martha through my friendship with the family."

Taking advantage of Martha! How could you tell this

uncomplicated American that nobody had ever, in all her life, taken advantage of Martha.

"What is your advice, Father?" Rodney Jackson asked him.

In his years as a priest he had found himself in some awkward situations, but this beat them all. He didn't have a notion! And yet this affable, charming man was sitting here looking at him, waiting for an answer. He decided to play for time.

"What had you in mind?" he enquired.

"Well, back home I would take her to a show and a meal, but you don't have those facilities here in Kilmeen," Rodney told him in a troubled voice.

Now, Tim thought, *where do we go from here?* Then he remembered something that Martha had mentioned in the confessional. Maybe there was a solution here.

"I think that I might have a suggestion," he began slowly.

"You do?"

"Well, it's only a suggestion now," Tim told him, not wanting to push this nice man into anything that he might regret.

"Let's have it," the American demanded.

"Well, you're going back to New York soon, and Mark is going with you for his exhibition. Right?"

"Right," Rodney confirmed.

"Why not invite his sister and niece along as well?" Tim suggested. "That would be quite in order, and then you would be on home ground."

"That's brilliant," Rodney Jackson declared, clapping his hands together. "A simply brilliant idea."

I hope he won't live to regret this enthusiasm, Tim thought, *but anyway the ball is in his field now, and at least Nora will have a smashing holiday.*

It defied his imagination to think of Martha and this man. A fine-looking man with a huge bank account apparently, but how would himself and Martha get on? This was a man who was used to running his own show. By all accounts, Martha had exercised a fair amount of control over Ned. This was going to be a different set up altogether. But then, maybe it might finish up as just a holiday.

"You're happy enough with that, so?" Tim asked.

"Delighted," he was told, "absolutely delighted, and I won't detain you another minute now, Father. I knew that you were the right man to come to. Priests are always wise in the ways of their parish."

If only they were, Tim thought; *if only they were.*

When Rodney Jackson was gone, Tim decided to make himself a cup of tea. It had been an eventful evening. He had always felt that he would not like to go up against Martha, but he had never in his wildest imagination thought of her as taking the law into her own hands like she had. She would never tell anybody, and he hoped that Danny Conway would get over the whole incident in time. Jack, Kate and Sarah would probably figure it out, but hopefully it would go no further than that. He dreaded to think of the outcome if

Rory Conway got hold of the details.

It would be interesting to know how Martha would react to Rodney Jackson's invitation. One could never be sure what way Martha would jump.

CHAPTER TWENTY-THREE

MARK HAD INVITED Rodney Jackson to Mossgrove for tea without even telling her about
it and Martha was extremely annoyed. It was
very out of character for Mark, who was a great believer in minding his own business and not interfering in
other people's lives. What on earth had prompted him
to invite Rodney Jackson to Mossgrove? Mark and himself were great friends, but she had very little in common with him.

She remembered him as a pampered little boy when
he had come as a child to visit his aunts. Then, of
course, years later he had come back as the great bene-
factor of Kilmeen. This tall, thin, tanned American
had also been the subject of great feminine interest in
Kilmeen, and Martha thought that he probably was a
bit full of himself.

But if Rodney Jackson was going to have tea in the parlour in Mossgrove, then she was not going to serve it in a room that was not up to scratch. The parlour was in the need of an overhaul. Always she had distempered the old walls, frowning at their irregularities, but now she decided that she was going to paper them. She returned in triumph from a visit to Ross with a heavy cream wallpaper embossed with a hint of pale rose. The price had made her cringe, but she was a firm believer that you had to pay for quality.

Martha began papering early one morning, and Nora took over in the kitchen. The one redeeming feature of Rodney Jackson's visit was that Nora, for the first time since Conway's attack on her, was showing some enthusiasm. The matching and hanging of the paper was tedious, but when Martha had a few strips up she knew that her choice was right. After the dinner her mother came and Nora, having finished in the kitchen, joined them and the three of them worked together.

"How's Ellen Shine?" Martha enquired of her mother.

"Oh, she's much better," Agnes answered, "almost back to her old self again. She really appreciated your calling to her."

"I like her because she has great mettle," Martha said.

"Ellen always had that," Agnes said. "She brought cutting into the Shines. They were always a bit on the slow side."

"You wouldn't exactly call Davy a speedy operator," Martha said wryly.

"Well, no," Agnes admitted, "but he's a sound little fellow all the same."

"Not so little," Nora remarked.

Agnes smiled and stood back to admire their efforts.

"Did you ever see such an improvement?" she asked. "It's like a different room. You payed for that paper, Martha."

"You can say that again," Martha told her, "but it was worth it, wasn't it?"

"Definitely," Agnes agreed.

"Mom, you have great taste," Nora told her quietly. She was still a long way from the old Nora, but at least she was showing interest in this undertaking.

Agnes was looking at the room with an appraising look on her face.

"I know exactly what this room needs," she stated. "I have a pair of rich curtains that the Miss Jacksons left to me in their will, beautiful heavy cream damask. I think that they were family heirlooms. They would be just right here. I'll measure the window and do whatever remodelling has to be done and bring them over tomorrow."

"Are you sure?" Martha asked doubtfully. "You have those in your trunk for years, and I always thought that you were saving them for something special."

"This is it," Agnes declared. "I always knew that one day I would find a home for them. This room is transformed now and just the right background."

"Well, I suppose the one good thing about Jackson's visit is that it made me look at this room with fresh eyes," Martha admitted, "though I still cannot understand why Mark decided to invite him."

"I have no idea," Agnes told her.

The following day Martha washed and polished the parlour floor. Old Edward had put down this floor and it was the devil to keep it looking well, but when it was polished, the rich glow was a compensation for the hard work. She polished the long sideboard and dining table and chairs. When the furniture was glowing, she stood and viewed the room. It looked good, but she needed something over the sideboard to balance the picture of Edward Phelan on the end wall. Many years ago when she came to Mossgrove, there had been a large gilt-framed portrait of Nellie Phelan hanging over the sideboard. *Americans are very interested in family history,* she thought. *I might as well give this American a view of the Phelan ancestral tree.*

She went upstairs and found the picture at the back of an old cupboard. There was Nellie's wedding photograph, and Kate and Ned as children with their parents, and smaller pictures of other Phelans. Carefully, she lifted out the heavy-framed pictures and unwrapped them. When she had put them away years previously, she had been very careful because the heavy gilt frames were so beautiful, but over the years the newspapers had yellowed and some had been torn away.

She brought them down to the kitchen and cleaned them carefully and then carried them up into the parlour. Slowly she hung them on the walls and smiled. The old nails were still there because to pull them out would have meant a shower of mortar accompanying them. It amused her that she was using the Phelans' portraits to impress Rodney Jackson. However, they certainly made the room more interesting.

The brass knob rattled and Peter put his head around the door, and when he saw the pictures he whistled in delighted surprise and then came fully into the room.

"I'm glad they're back," he said appreciatively. "I often opened that cupboard upstairs and felt that they were part of our family relegated to the attic."

"You never said."

"No, they were better off above if they were not welcome down here," he told her.

She knew by Peter's tone of voice that he was not trying to annoy her. Despite all their clashes, there was between the two of them a strong bond, as if they were hewn off the same rock. He was direct and strong and deserved nothing but the truth. Maybe the time for truth had come. She walked over to the photograph of Nellie Phelan and, looking up at her, said thoughtfully, "I think that I may have wronged that woman."

He came across the room and put his arm around her shoulder. "It takes honesty and courage to admit it," he told her.

"Courage must be in the air around here these days," she said ruefully.

The special tea was to be on Sunday and Martha spent Saturday getting ready. She had killed and plucked two large cockerels, and as they were having the supper on Saturday night, the smell of herbs and stuffing filled the kitchen.

The following day when Martha had all in readiness, she stood back to admire the parlour. Agnes's beautiful curtains billowed to the floor in a foam of creamy waves. She had really surpassed herself in her imaginative creation, with matching cushions on the low window seat and the old shutters painted the same shade as the curtains. The whole window area poured brightness into the parlour, which was continued in Martha's rich cream wallpaper. For the first time ever, she thought that the old oak furniture was enriched and shown to advantage. Agnes had really brought a new dimension to the room, and with the leftover material she had made matching cushion covers for the dining room chairs. Martha had often been tempted to throw out Nellie Phelan's down cushions, and now she was glad that she had held on to them because, with the new cream covers, they draped over the black leather seats of the oak chairs and softened their appearance. The long sideboard and the black marble fireplace were laden with vases of Nellie Phelan's Gallic roses that filled the air with their rich musky essence, and arching ferns stretched themselves out of the deep fire grate and contrasted vividly with the black marble. The entire effect was a room full of light and elegance.

Martha was glad that she had hung the old pictures because the deep gilt frames were rich against the pale paper, but apart from the fact that they enhanced the room, the effect on Peter was surprising. Over the years it had not occured to her that he had resented the fact that the pictures were upstairs. *Sometimes though living in the same house,* she thought, *we do not always know what is going on in each other's heads.*

Jack was first to arrive and stood gazing at the room in silence as Martha watched and wondered what he was thinking. He walked over to the picture of Nellie and looked up at it, and suddenly it came to her with blinding clarity that Jack had loved this woman. What a lifetime of dedication to a woman and a place. She went across the room and put her hand on his shoulder, and when he turned towards her his eyes were full of tears.

"We've come a long way, Jack," she said quietly.

"We have indeed, Martha," he smiled through his tears, "and some of that journey took a lot of guts."

She knew then that he knew the story of Yalla Hole and she was glad. The knowledge that Jack knew and was standing with her was a comfort.

Kate arrived soon after and stopped short at the door of the parlour.

"Oh," she gasped, "the pictures are back and the whole room is quite beautiful."

"Nana Agnes did the curtains," Nora told her.

"They're exquisite," Kate said, fingering the heavy material and tracing the embossed satin designs with her fingers.

"They came out of the Miss Jackson's old house," Martha told her.

"How extraordinary that they will be hanging here now for their nephew's first visit to Mossgrove. Well, you've really transformed the place," Kate declared warmly, "and it's good to see the pictures back."

"They belong here," Peter said, "and now we are going to get Uncle Mark to paint Mom's and Dad's wedding picture, and we'll put it up as well."

"I never thought of that," Martha said in surprise. It was good to hear it coming from Peter.

"Rodney is gone back to collect Mark and Agnes," Kate told them.

"I can't understand why Mark invited him here," Martha declared.

"But it's lovely, isn't it?" Nora said.

"A bit of a family get-together is always nice," Kate agreed.

"Well he's not exactly family," Martha objected.

"I suppose he is in a way, because his aunts, the Miss Jacksons, were distantly related to your family," Kate told her.

"I'm not exactly family either," Jack smiled.

"You're more than that, Jack," Kate told him. "You're the heart of the whole place."

"Davy would have been here as well," Peter told him, "but you know that his mother has an old aunt home on holiday and she insisted that Davy be there for the dinner."

A few minutes later they heard a car in the yard and Peter announced, "The Yank is here."

"Don't call him that," Nora objected.

"Well, they all call him that in the village," Peter told her.

"Well, we're not the village," Nora asserted with some of her old spirit.

Just then there was a knock on the door and they all stared at each other in surprise.

"God," Peter declared, voicing all their thoughts, "we're getting very formal around here."

Hurrying into the porch, Martha opened the front door and had a huge bunch of flowers thrust into her arms.

"For the lady of the house," Rodney Jackson announced.

Martha was completely taken aback. It was the first time that she had ever been presented with a formal bouquet of flowers and she was rendered momentarily speechless, but Nora had no such problem.

"Oh, aren't they simply gorgeous?" she exclaimed, burying her nose in them and taking them from her mother. "What a lovely surprise."

"Come in, come in," Martha told them, regaining her composure, and Agnes and Mark followed

Rodney Jackson into the parlour. He looked around in delight.

"What a room!" he enthused.

"It's lovely, isn't it?" Nora told him. "We did it up specially for you."

"How wonderful, and excuse me for saying so, but this is one superb set-up. Look at those drapes."

"They actually came out of your aunts' old home," Agnes told him, and his face lit up with pleasure.

"How extraordinary," he said.

"They gave them to me years ago," Agnes told him, "and it looks as if they were designed for this room."

"It's almost as if the aunts are here to welcome me," he said thoughtfully. He wandered around the room looking at the photographs, but suddenly turned around to apologise.

"I'm being very rude staring at your family portraits, but they are just great."

Well, at least I got that right, Martha thought ironically as she retrieved the flowers from Nora and took them to the kitchen to stand in water until she could arrange them later. They were a spectacular collection and she wondered, *Where on earth did he buy them? Must have cost him a pretty penny,* but it was a nice feeling to be at the receiving end of such a bouquet. She gave herself time in the kitchen to recover her composure.

When she returned to the parlour, Rodney Jackson was standing in front of Nellie Phelan's portrait and commenting, "Nora, you are so like her."

"But she is lovely," Nora protested.

"But so are you, my dear," he drawled and she blushed with pleasure.

There was no doubt but that he was good for Nora.

As they stood around the room chatting, Martha realised that Rodney Jackson had everyone totally at ease in his company. He was a very charming man. Nora obviously thought that he was perfect and Agnes seemed to regard him as a second son, while to Mark and Kate he was a trusted friend. Peter alone was sizing him up with a quizzical look on his face. *I'm a bit like Peter,* Martha decided, *not so sure if this fellow is as perfect as he is painted.* He certainly looked good with his close-cropped dark hair and sallow complexion. She liked his lean look and decided that you could compare him to one of Davy Shine's greyhounds, not carrying a spare pound but yet conveying a determined strength. He looked far younger than his age, which she had calculated must be at the wrong side of forty.

"Let's all be seated," Martha announced, drawing back the chairs, "and, Kate, as the original Phelan in the room, we'll give you the head of the table." She was amused to witness Kate's expression and to see Peter cast a startled glance in her own direction.

"Peter, you take the other end," she told him, "and, Rodney, you sit here inside the table from where you can look down over the fields. Nora and Jack, you take these chairs beside him. Mark, Agnes and I will sit opposite."

When they were all seated, Rodney Jackson looked around appreciatively.

"That's what I'd call a good seating arrangement," he said, smiling at Martha, and she got the feeling that beneath this extremely pleasant exterior was a sharp brain that missed very little. She liked that. There was nothing more boring than fools.

Nora had decided to act as hostess and passed around plates of roast chicken salad that her mother had ready. Martha was glad that she had taken so much trouble in the preparation of everything. It had brought Nora into the spirit of things. Nothing was more important than that just now.

"Mark, you're a lucky skunk heading off to America," Peter announced from the end of the table. "When exactly are you leaving?"

"As soon as things are organised," said Rodney.

"You had better mind him in America," Peter told Rodney good humouredly. "He could get lost, wander off after strange women or something."

"More likely strange butterflies," Martha put in.

"Wouldn't I love to be going?" Nora said wistfully.

"Why not?" Rodney Jackson asked her.

"What?" Nora gasped in disbelief.

"Well, now that it has come up, it seems like a good time to tell you that that is why I'm here, to invite you and your mother to accompany us and see Mark's exhibition for yourselves."

There was a stunned silence at the table. Then

everybody started talking together, and Nora was on her feet hugging Rodney and Mark and running around the table to Agnes, Kate and Jack. Amazement followed by understanding flooded though Martha. *So this is what the invitation to Mossgrove was all about.* She turned and looked at Mark beside her.

"You knew all along," she said.

"Yes. The change will be great for Nora, just what she needs, and it will do you good to get away as well."

His tone of voice was such that for one second she wondered if he knew about that night at the river. Mark wandered around at the oddest hours. It was not outside the limits of possibility that he had been out that night. On impulse she took his hand and squeezed it.

"Thank you," she said simply.

"This is a big surprise," she told Rodney. "Do we have to decide straightaway?"

"You can think about it," he told her.

"Think about it!" Nora shrieked. "There is no thinking to be done. We're going and that's it."

The effect on Nora was amazing. She was vibrating with excitement and delight.

"Well, there seems to be no decision to be made," Martha smiled, "but of course there will be certain arrangements to be made."

"I'm looking after Mossgrove and Ellen Shine will help," Agnes told her.

"So you knew too?" Martha asked.

"Only because they had to tell me on account of covering Mossgrove while you're away. It was all very hush-hush."

"Once I get over the initial shock, I'm sure that I will be as delighted as Nora," Martha said.

"You couldn't be, Mam," Nora declared, dancing around the room. "I'm on air."

The rest of the meal was given over to making plans and arrangements, with Nora giving Agnes instructions about clothes that would have to be made for her. Agnes was in for a busy time, but it was so good to see the transformation in Nora. Martha would always be grateful to Mark for this.

Now that Rodney Jackson had made his announcement, he appeared to be happy to sit back and let the conversation flow around him. It would be interesting to know how he really felt about Nora and herself accompanying Mark. Was he doing it just to humour Mark, whom he thought, for some strange reason, should have his every wish answered? Was it his idea or was it Mark's? It would be nice to know, but she doubted that she was going to find out in the immediate future.

They all enjoyed the meal and were loud in their praise of Martha's cooking. Sometimes when she looked across the table, she found Rodney Jackson's eyes on her. It was a bit disconcerting. She wondered how they would get on during the long trip ahead. There was a lot more to this man than met the eye.

Later that evening she stood alone inside the parlour window and looked across at Conways'. They were no longer a threat to Mossgrove. Looking down over the fields, she thought of all the generations of Phelans who had worked this farm. Now they were gone, but Mossgrove remained. Maybe Jack was right and none of them owned this land.

She walked over and looked up at the picture of old Edward Phelan. For the first time in twenty-two years, she felt a complete affinity with a Phelan.

"The score is settled," she told him.